Kenny Evans is in the fifth grade. He's a gifted student and has a great teacher and great friends. Sure, his little sister can be a pain, and his grandmother smokes too much, but overall he has no complaints.

Then one day his dad loses his job and is forced to start a new one. Suddenly everything changes - even the way his friends feel about him – and Kenny is living a nightmare.

Kenny has a lot on his mind. If he could just quit feeling so angry and ashamed, maybe he could figure out what to do. And then, in the most unlikely place on the planet he meets Lydia. And she has a clue.

Kenny's story is one that will resonate with anyone who was ever caught in the middle of a situation beyond their control. The second in a classroom series, this story hits home and will not be quickly forgotten.

⌘

Not This Sunday

by
Cindy Lovell

*With a foreword by Nicholas Colangelo, Professor
and Director of the Belin-Blank Center for Gifted
Education at The University of Iowa*

N.L. Associates, Inc.

PO Box 1199

Hightstown, NJ 08520-0399

ISBN 978-1-878347-72-5

Printed in the United States of America

This book is affectionately dedicated to
Mr. Ronald E. Riese, my fourth grade teacher at
Newberry Elementary School who introduced me
to the writings of Mark Twain. Thanks, Mr. Riese!

⌘

Special thanks to the students of
Mrs. Margaret Crayne's class and to the students of
Mrs. Elaine Beeghley's class for their
enthusiasm and devotion to reading.

⌘

More special thanks to Christopher Finkle
for his help with the cover.

Foreword

Cindy Lovell doesn't write about kids, she brings them to your heart. Cindy loves kids: otherwise the characters of Kenny, Lydia, and Rachel would not be possible. She also loves education and the thrill of learning; otherwise, Mrs. Juarez would not be possible. Fortunately, they all become part of us.

Cindy has a wonderful sense of kids struggling with things at home that they can't fully grasp but can fully feel. She captured this in *Rachel Mason Hears the Sound* and again in *Not This Sunday*.

Also, Cindy captures, in quite a gentle but powerful way, what is means to be a gifted child. Kenny and Rachel are very bright, sensitive to what they do and don't understand, and caring of those around them. The giftedness in a child simply flows through the life of that child.

Cindy is a writer who attends to emotional detail. Children will love to read *Not This Sunday* and so will anyone who hasn't forgotten.

Nicholas Colangelo

Table of Contents

Chapter 1 – You are an Alligator!

Kenny daydreamed. He remembered the time his dad made pancakes on the griddle by pouring the batter in the shapes of animals. Kenny smiled as he recalled the snake. It wiggled across the length of the griddle and broke apart when his dad tried to flip it. Still, it was fun, and everyone ate a piece of the "snake" for breakfast.

"Kenny?" His teacher's voice jerked him back to the class discussion. What were they talking about now? "Rachel had fresh squeezed orange juice," Mrs. Juarez smiled at Kenny. "Where would we find that on the food pyramid?" Oh, great, they were still talking about breakfast, but he had no idea what Mrs. Juarez was trying to get out of him. "Where does orange juice come from?"

Relieved, a semi-panicked Kenny put it together in the nick of time to keep from looking like a complete idiot in front of the class. "Fruits!" he exclaimed. There, that ought to do it.

"Absolutely!" praised Mrs. Juarez. "Orange juice is made from oranges, so Rachel's fresh squeezed orange juice would go in the 'Fruits' category." Mrs. Juarez was off and running, lecturing about the newest topic – nutrition. Kenny drifted back to that morning his dad cooked breakfast.

"Is this great or what?" his dad asked.

"Make me a frog!" squealed Annette, Kenny's little sister.

"Okay! Abracadabra! You are a *frog!*" Mr. Evans waved the spatula like a wand.

"Oh, *you* know what I mean! Make me a frog pancake!"

Everyone laughed at the misshapen frog formed from the pancake batter. It looked more like a frog that had been squashed on the road, but Annette eagerly speared it with her fork and made faces while she took huge bites of the imaginary amphibian.

"Look! Annette's eating *frog legs!*" Kenny laughed. Annette chewed with her mouth open as though she was trying to see. Part of the pancake fell out of her mouth onto her plate.

"Gross!" Kenny averted his eyes from the semi-chewed frog legs.

"Kenny!" Annette snorted. "You made me spit it out."

And so it went: Mr. Evans pouring different shapes, Mrs. Evans offering encouragement and suggestions. Kenny broke up pieces of his bacon and stuck them in for eyes.

"Remember the time we made pancakes at the park?" his mom asked wistfully.

"Oh, let's go back there!" Annette coaxed. "They had blueberries for eyes," she stated emphatically, "and chocolate chips." Annette reached up with syrup-sticky fingers and pulled a strand of curly blonde hair out of her eyes.

"Yeah… Can we go back there again?" Kenny asked. De Leon Springs State Park was the favorite of all the state parks he had ever visited. The little restaurant there had griddles built into every table, and you were able to cook your own pancakes.

"I don't know," kidded his mom. "They make you cook your own breakfast there! What kind of place is that?" Kenny knew she wasn't serious. Whenever friends or relatives visited from out of the area that was one of the places his mom liked to take them. It was a beautiful park with a swimming area over the spring. You could rent canoes and go paddling, too. They often saw alligators. Annette must have been remembering the same thing.

"Make me an alligator, Daddy!"

"Okay! Abracadabra! You are an *alligator*!" Dad beamed while Annette groaned. Ron Evans never minded laughing at himself.

Kenny sighed and felt a painful sadness at the memory. He turned his attention back to his teacher and the other students. He loved being in Mrs. Juarez's class. If she caught students going to "La La Land" as she called it, she didn't embarrass them by pointing it out. Instead, she propped them up and brought them back into the discussion. Her kindness was not lost on Kenny. He knew she had just saved him with her question about oranges.

As the other students talked about serving sizes and balanced meals, Kenny's interest in the lesson waned. The class discussion about breakfast kept returning him to that morning almost one year ago when his dad made the animal-shaped pancakes. His eyes glazed over, grew moist. Kenny swallowed several times, which somehow helped hold his tears in. He looked at the clock. DEAR time would soon begin. Mrs. Juarez was never late for DEAR time – Drop Everything And Read. He fumbled in his desk for a distraction – anything would do - and gripped a two-inch pencil nub that would no longer fit in the pencil sharpener.

Kenny rolled the little pencil in his fingers, averting his eyes from his classmates, hoping he wouldn't be called on. His head bent forward, Kenny's thin frame looked small and vulnerable. Mrs. Juarez glanced at Kenny. Although she was unable to catch his gaze, she intuitively sensed his despair, and understood. Sometimes La La Land wasn't such a bad thing, she thought, and announced DEAR time.

In less than sixty seconds Kenny and his classmates had settled themselves with a reading selection of their choice. For the next fifteen minutes students would be lost in the words of a favorite author or a newly discovered one. DEAR time was considered precious, and the fifth graders of Mrs. Juarez's class did not squander a second of it. Kenny removed the Harry Potter bookmark from his own book, *Hoot*, by Carl Hiaasen. Mrs. Juarez had recommended it, and he identified with Roy, the main character. In a few minutes, Kenny's own troubles dissipated as he focused on Roy's latest dilemma concerning Mullet Fingers. Five minutes, ten minutes, oh, how this class hated for DEAR time to end. Kenny was too engaged in the adventure to notice the clock, but his reverie ended suddenly when he saw the school's D.A.R.E. officer walk by on his way to Mrs. Mercer's class.

Officer Randall nodded a greeting in the general direction of the unnoticing students who were spread out and sprawled under desks or on bean bag chairs. Even Mrs. Juarez, reading an *Instructor* magazine, didn't notice as he strode down the sidewalk outside their classroom. Only Kenny saw him. Saw his uniform, saw his badge, saw his look of authority, and saw – how out of place it looked! – the kind smile on the D.A.R.E. officer's face. The tears Kenny had bravely held in earlier now spilled onto the pages of *Hoot*, which he gripped tightly, hoping desperately not to be noticed. Another long day awaited.

C hapter 2 – Gram Sitting

When the bell rang at the end of the day, Kenny bolted out the door, relieved to be heading home. He didn't know what was wrong with him. He *hated* crying in school, and felt thankful no one had noticed his tears earlier in the day. Unbeknownst to him, Mrs. Juarez's watchful eyes *had* noticed. That DEAR time lasted an extra five minutes was no accident. As she watched him wrestle with his emotions, Mrs. Juarez longed to comfort Kenny. However, she instinctively sensed that he needed this private moment. Allowing the class to go on reading uninterrupted gave Kenny time to regain his composure. She remembered a professor in college who cautioned her along with all of the would-be teachers in her class: *Your students will bring every possible sorrow and joy into your classrooms. Many simply cannot leave their troubles at the classroom door.* How often Jane Juarez had remembered those words throughout her teaching career, and today was one of those days. Now school was over and everyone could let their breath out.

"Mom! Look what I did!" Annette called, waving a colorful hodgepodge as she bounced down the sidewalk. "It's my magical signature!" she pronounced proudly. "See? We painted our names in the middle, on the line, and then when we folded them they were magical." Annette beamed.

"You mean, 'symmetrical'," corrected Kenny.

"Yeah. Smagical."

"Remember, Mom, I made one in Mrs. Morton's class, too?" Kenny asked.

"I remember. I still have it." Maggie Evans grabbed the half-crumpled painting and smoothed it out on the steering wheel of the family's well-worn minivan.

"It's bee-yoo-tee-full, Annette!" She always said *bee-yoo-tee-full* that way to Annette, to imitate the way Annette always sounded.

"I'll have to find Kenny's, and we'll put them both on display." Kenny thought Annette's little painting looked something like a fence with the double Ns and double Ts. A shaky fence. He couldn't remember what his own symmetrical signature looked like and felt a surprising surge of pride that his mom had kept it.

"We have to hurry. I'm sorry, kids, but I have to go in early tonight. Gram's gonna stay over."

Both children were silent, each thinking their own thoughts. They loved their Gram, and tended to look past her propensity for complaining about everything and everybody. They even looked past her nasty cigarette smoking habit most of the time. But lately she seemed even grouchier than usual. Kenny could see the worried look in his mom's eyes. Sure enough, Annette started to whine.

"Gram is too grouchy." Annette always cut to the chase. "She makes me grouchy, too."

Mrs. Evans pulled up to a stoplight and looked in the rearview mirror at Annette. Beseechingly she asked, "Honey, please behave for Gram. Maybe you can show her how to make a symmetrical signature!" She tried to sound hopeful, but the tension in her voice suggested resignation that Annette was about to pitch one of her memorable fits

– now, just when she had to go to work. Kenny had been paying attention. He never coaxed Annette like everyone else did.

"Annette," he asked, changing the subject, "did you guys do calculator math yet in Mrs. Morton's class?"

"No. What's that?" Annette promptly dropped the whole Gram negotiations.

"Aw, you're kidding! She didn't show you all the words you can write on a calculator? Okay... I'll show you tonight. Then when Mrs. Morton goes to teach you, you'll already be an expert." This suited Annette. She smiled smugly and leaned back into the worn seat. Kenny met his mom's gaze. She silently thanked him with a smile.

"Can we go to McDonald's?" Annette was a connoisseur of chicken nuggets, and McDonald's was her first choice.

"Sorry, honey, I promise we'll go soon. Gram's making supper for you."

"I don't mean for supper. I mean for a snack."

"No, not today…" Mom's voice trailed off in a distracted way.

Mrs. Evans slowed to make a turn. A Sheriff's deputy had someone pulled over, probably a speeder. Kenny looked at his mom and saw her grip the wheel a little tighter. Although her eyes were on the road, Maggie Evans seemed to avert them downward. Even her body appeared to shrink in the presence of the officer alongside the road. Kenny remembered his reaction at seeing Officer Randall at school today and thought, *Even Mom is afraid of seeing the cops.* Life sure had been turned upside down for the Evans family.

Up ahead Kenny saw their house, his grandmother's car parked in the driveway. Well, technically it wasn't really a house, he thought, but a mobile home. A double-wide. A *trailer* was what Gram called it, with great disdain as though her daughter and grandchildren lived in an old car at the junkyard, and as if they did it just to spite her. The truth was their place was modest, but neat and tidy and surprisingly spacious for a "trailer." Kenny wasn't embarrassed to have friends over. In fact, some of his friends' houses weren't this nice. So why Gram yapped about it was a mystery to him. He had his own room with built-in bookshelves and a desk, and even his own bathroom. Of course, Gram found fault in just about everything. Kenny had learned to shrug off her negative attitude most of the time.

"Okay, kids, I love you. Be sure to do your homework and chores, and be nice to Gram. I don't get off 'til ten-thirty, but I'll sneak a peak and make sure you're dreaming sweet dreams when I get home. Mmmmpwah…" she kissed Annette as Annette's little arms circled her neck for a hug. Kenny leaned over and kissed his mom. He wouldn't do this in front of his friends, but at home it was different.

Both kids hopped out and stood and watched as their mom put the minivan in reverse. She waved as she backed out of their gravel driveway and headed to her cashier's job at the Publix grocery store. As she rounded the corner and drove out of sight, Kenny and Annette turned and braced for the inevitable confrontation with their mother's mother. It was bound to go something like this:

"Gram, look at my picture!"

"What's-it-s'pose-tuh-be?   Gram always ran her
words together.

"A smagical!"

"It's Annette's symmetrical signature, Gram.
See?" Kenny would explain and demonstrate. "Mom
says she still has the one I made in first grade."

"That's-yer-mom-alright,   cough-cough-cough,
always-hangin-onto-junk,   cough-cough,   *just-look-at-his-
place…"* and she'd gesture with her cigarette, fat ashes
flying as she flailed her flabby arm, indicating
imaginary piles of filthy garbage. Kenny would try to
be nice, and Annette would go watch TV.   The
scenario would vary slightly in the subject matter, but
the tone was always the same.

As Kenny began to turn the knob on the
door, something made him listen. No, it wasn't
Gram's usual hacking smoker's cough. What was it?
Annette heard it and paused, too. There it was again.
Gaaahhhh… followed by a drawn out muffled sound.
Kenny gingerly opened the door, not sure what he
expected to see. Both kids stood frozen in their
tracks. There sat Gram, semi-slumped over in their
dad's old La-Z-Boy recliner, head in her hands! *Oh*

no, Kenny thought, *she's having a heart attack!* He and Annette both gaped at the sight of their grandmother, too stunned to move for a split second.

"Well-what-are-yuh-lookin-at?" she snapped, shocking them both. They stared, speechless. Gram blew her nose loudly and wiped her eyes on her sleeve.

"What," she bellowed again, *"are-yuh-lookin-at?"* And as she rose to her feet, taking a deep drag on her cigarette, Kenny and Annette slowly realized that she wasn't having a heart attack at all. Gram had simply been sitting there crying her eyes out!

C hapter 3 – Collect Call

As Kenny and Annette collected their wits, Gram crushed her cigarette out in an ashtray and made her way to the kitchen. *"I'll-get-yer-dinner-started."*

While neither child was especially fond of Gram's griping, both were disquieted at this new side of Gram. It disturbed them to catch her crying like that. This was certainly an unpredictable turn of events, and neither was sure how to proceed. Annette resolved it by heading for the TV and turning it on. She climbed into her dad's recliner recently vacated by Gram and began channel surfing. *Clifford* was usually on when they got home, and she liked to curl up to watch the big red dog.

Kenny decided to get his homework out of the way. Mrs. Juarez had assigned the writing of a poem. This was definitely not Kenny's strongest talent. He much preferred writing stories. But this poem was supposed to be about his favorite food, so that made it more interesting. There was a math assignment, too, so he would get that out of the way first. Mrs. Juarez also asked everyone to bring in some kind of food label for the unit on nutrition they were starting. Kenny didn't really want to go into the kitchen asking Gram for a label. He could do that in the morning before school when his mom would be there and Gram would be gone.

Mrs. Juarez made math easy for Kenny. He used to struggle with it, but no more. He had learned to calculate percentages and loved it when he went to Wal-Mart with his mom. Eavesdropping on grownups around the clearance racks try to calculate the sale prices gave him a great sense of pride in mastering this particular skill.

"How much is twenty-five percent off?"

"I don't know. What's the regular price?"

"$24.99"

"Well, it will be a couple dollars. I don't know...? Maybe three or four."

And that's how it would go. Kenny loved being able to do this in his head with the tricks Mrs. Juarez, a big believer in mental math, had taught them. In fact, when they'd line up to go to special area, like art or music, she would pose one long, drawn out, mental math problem as they walked along. Everyone would calculate it in their heads, and if Mr. Joseph, the principal, passed by on the sidewalk he would always exclaim, "Mrs. Juarez, no other class has such a straight and quiet line!" Then he'd go on, beaming with pride, and no doubt wishing that all of his teachers knew how to line up students like Mrs. Juarez. And all the while they were silently working on one great math problem. Mrs. Juarez was the only one talking – everyone in the class listened carefully and did mental calculations.

"What is twenty minus four…" pause to calculate, "…divided by four…" pause to calculate, "…plus fourteen…"and on it would go until they reached their destination. Every single student wanted to be called on to answer, and rarely did anyone get it wrong.

So, Kenny sailed through his math homework and then started to think about his favorite food poem. He sighed deeply. Poetry just wasn't his thing. Not even a poem about his favorite food. Still, he wanted to please Mrs. Juarez. She always made you feel like you could succeed at anything – even writing a poem about your favorite food. He really didn't know what to write. Truthfully, he just didn't care. He had far more important matters on his mind these days. Just then Gram called that dinner was ready.

"Come-and-get-it-kids!" she croaked in her raspy voice. Brother and sister joined Gram in the bright little kitchen. They preferred eating at the snack bar rather than the dining room table. It afforded a better view of the TV in the living room.

"Grilled-cheese-sandwiches-and-vegetable-soup," Gram announced. It was impossible now to tell that she had ever been crying. Annette seemed to have forgotten altogether as she focused her attention between her sandwich and the remote control. Kenny, though, found himself scrutinizing his grandmother for signs of trouble. He watched Gram pick up her own sandwich and begin to chew. At least she didn't smoke while she ate. Gram's short, permed hair was dyed black and today was needing combed. She wore no cosmetics, although she usually distinguished herself with a tube of Royal Red

lipstick by Revlon. Not today, though. She wore bright red shorts and a white pullover top that had "OBX" across the front in black, a testament to her favorite place in the world – the Outer Banks of North Carolina. Sometimes, Kenny thought, his grandmother didn't really look or act very grandmotherly. She reached down and scratched a mosquito bite on her ankle. She was wearing flip-flops. But this was Florida, and everyone wore flip-flops.

"*Whatcha-thinkin-about?*" she directed at Kenny.

"Nothing," he lied. Great! Now she was becoming a mind-reader. Kenny turned his attention to the grilled cheese sandwich with renewed interest. He really wasn't in the mood to converse with Gram anyway. This whole day had been something of a trial so far. He tried to think about a favorite food poem. Suddenly writing a poem seemed very inviting – or rather, distracting.

"*You-should-get-outside-and-play,*" Gram barked at him. This was her way of making conversation.

"I have homework."

"You-look-pale-to-me," she observed. Gram was somewhat obsessed with having a "great tan." *"How-can-you-live-in-Florida-looking-so-pale?"* She had finished her sandwich and was lighting a fresh cigarette. *Gross!* Kenny knew his clothes smelled like an ashtray whenever Gram watched them. Why couldn't his mom trust him to keep an eye on Annette? Why couldn't they stay home alone? Gulping the last spoonful of soup, Kenny stood up and took his dishes to the sink. He quickly rinsed them and put them in the dishwasher.

"I'm gonna finish my homework, Gram," he called over his shoulder. "I'll do my chores in a little while."

Thirty minutes later Kenny was still agonizing over his poem. Or rather, he was agonizing in general. The poem was his justification to feel frustrated and even a little angry. *What a stupid assignment anyway*, he thought. *Who cares about a favorite food poem?* He felt hostile towards Mrs. Juarez. Big deal, they were going to learn about nutrition. What good is nutrition when your grandmother pollutes everyone around her with her smelly cancer sticks?

Why bother learning about good nutrition when your own grandmother was killing you off one puff of secondhand smoke at a time?

The ringing of the phone broke the spell. Kenny sat still for a minute, then ran to the kitchen. He watched his grandmother listen to the receiver, then saw her press "1" to accept the collect call. *"Hiya-Ron, Maggie's-at-work, she-had-to-go-in-early, uh-huh,uh-huh, yes, uh-huh…"* She handed the phone to Kenny who was standing as still as a statue, waiting.

"It's-yer-dad… He-wants-to-talk-to-you."

Kenny walked silently and quickly across the linoleum floor. Annette clamored out of her dad's chair and came shrieking into the kitchen.

"I wanna talk to Daddy!"

"It's Kenny's turn," Gram told Annette gently - patiently - taking Annette's chubby little hand and leading her down the hall so Kenny could hear. Gram spoke carefully. "You'll get a turn, but please be quiet while Kenny gets *his* turn."

"Hullo?" Kenny spoke softly.

"Kenny! Hello, son! How's my boy? How are you?"

"Fine. I'm fine, Dad. How are you?" Kenny wound the cord tightly around his wrist, wrapping and unwrapping it as he talked. His voice was steady and measured.

"I'm just fine, son." His dad always called him, "son." It made Kenny sad to hear it now. "How's school? What are you doing in school?" The questions were easy, but the conversation was hard.

"School's good. We're writing a favorite food poem. I was thinking about the time you made animal pancakes." Kenny regretted saying it immediately.

"Oh, that's a great idea! I can't wait to read it! You'll send me a copy, won't you?"

"Yeah. And we'll be studying nutrition, too." Suddenly Kenny felt at a loss for words. There was so much Kenny wanted to tell his dad, but there was no easy way to begin.

"How's your mom?" Kenny could hear the apprehension in his dad's voice. Life was so unfair! "I was hoping to catch her before she went in."

"Mom got called in early," Kenny explained. "She's fine."

"When's it my turn?" demanded Annette, suddenly flying into the kitchen like a puppy off its leash, Gram close behind. "I want to talk to Daddy!"

"Dad, Annette wants..."

You have one minute of time remaining. The recorded voice on the phone interrupted Kenny.

"What? What did you say, son? I only have a minute." His voice was panicked.

"Annette wants her turn to talk," Kenny told him quickly.

"Okay, put her on. I love you, son. Help Mom. I know you are. I'm really proud of you son. *Really* proud! I love you!"

"I love you, too, Dad."

Kenny relinquished the phone to Annette who launched into a detailed report about her "smagical" signature with a promise to make a special one for her dad. As Dad tried to explain that there was no time left to talk, the connection was lost. Annette never understood this.

"Call Daddy back, Gram. I didn't finish telling him something."

"We can't call him, honey." Gram spoke slowly and put her cigarette in the ashtray and pulled Annette into her lap. "We have to let him call us when he can." Annette sighed. She looked in between a pout and a cry. Gram thought fast.

"Now-how-bout-we-write-him-a-letter? Okay? Okay? Wanna-make-that-magical-signature-for'im?" Kenny felt proud of Gram. Sure, Gram could be grouchy, but she definitely looked out for him and Annette. Gram saw the sadness in Kenny's face and reached out with Annette on her lap, pulling him in for a hug. *"Yer-dad's-proud-of-ya, and-so-am-I,"* she tried to reassure him. Her tender mood caught him off guard. Kenny's nerves were raw, and hearing his dad's faraway voice over the collect call did not help. For the second time that day hot tears ran uncontrollably down his face. Kenny buried his head against Gram, oblivious to the smell of cigarettes, and sobbed.

Chapter 4 – Quiet Evening

Thirty minutes later Kenny was back in his room. He felt exhausted, but took a long, deep breath. The crying had helped. Kenny still felt sad – he would *always* be sad – but he felt better. Gram and Annette were seated at the snack bar working on Annette's symmetrical signature for Dad. Annette was going to teach Gram how to make one, too. Kenny's feet dangled off the edge of the bed as he absentmindedly scanned the bedroom. The familiar sight of bookshelves full of books and souvenirs soothed him. Trophies, video games, and sports equipment filled every nook and cranny.

Kenny's parents weren't rich. Still, his stuff was nice – as nice as anyone's. But now times were different, and he wondered if they would ever be able to buy nice things again. Heck, half the kids in his class were on free and reduced lunch. What was he worrying about? At least he could afford lunch.

Kenny remembered back in third grade that after winter break a new student had joined the class who lived in his car with his parents and two sisters. They actually lived in their car! The thought of this made Kenny shudder as he imagined how it would feel to give up his home and live in his mom's minivan with her and Annette. He sat very still and pondered what it must have been like for that family. They moved after a few weeks, and Kenny occasionally wondered what had become of them.

Kenny's gaze lingered on a photo collage his mom had made. There was baby Kenny, fat and sassy and grinning at his dad who held him awkwardly but proudly. And there was little boy Kenny carefully holding his squinty-eyed new sister on his lap. Other pictures showed him wearing his T-ball "uniform" – a bright green T-shirt with the sponsor's name – Family Orthodonics – misspelled on the back and one of his favorites, a picture taken from behind on his first trip to Disney World. He was wearing mouse ears with "Kenny" embroidered across the back, holding Dad's hand. Mom must have taken this picture as they were leaving the theme park. It was on Kenny's fourth birthday, a long time ago, but he remembered it vividly. Aunt Amy had bought the ears for him. And there was a picture of the family at De Leon Springs State Park, in front of the big water wheel. No doubt they were on one of their pancake-making expeditions.

Pancakes! Kenny had to tackle the poem assignment. Grabbing his tablet and flopping across the bed diagonally, Kenny jotted down a few words. He had promised to send his dad a copy. Now he really wanted to do a good job. Hmmmm... Pancakes. *In the mood for favorite food, pancakes take the cake...* Not bad, not bad. He really wanted to write about the animal shapes. Clever poetry writing just wasn't his forte. He struggled, wrote, reflected, erased, read and re-read, and finally said, "There!"

Kenny stretched. It was late, and tiredness was setting in. He hadn't even done his chores yet. As Kenny got up he wondered why it was so quiet. Kenny walked softly out into the hallway. A program played on TV, although the volume was turned low. Instinctively he knew both Gram and Annette had fallen asleep with the TV on. Sure enough, they were stretched out on the couch, curly-headed Annette snuggled up next to their grandmother who was snoring lightly, while on the TV screen a heavily made-up middle-aged woman dramatically confided to someone, "I'm afraid I've become a - *shopaholic!*" Kenny, feeling all alone yet very responsible and in charge, turned off the TV before the woman's confidante could confess her deepest, darkest secret. Kenny thought of Haley Bennington at school. She often professed to being a shopaholic. It seemed to him to be strictly a girl issue.

When Kenny took the trash out he was careful not to accidentally lock himself out as just about everyone in his family had done at some time or another. The lock on the kitchen door could be tricky. Moving quickly and quietly, Kenny soon had everything done – laundry put away, trash carried out, and the dishwasher unloaded. Kenny had to be extra careful to do this quietly. He especially didn't want to disturb his sister and grandmother now. Annette would be sufficiently rested to remember Kenny's promise with the calculator, but he was more interested in sleeping than showing Annette that an upside-down 4 looked like the letter "h."

An hour or so later Maggie Evans punched out, tired but happy. The cash register had come out even, and Maggie was one of the first to leave. She didn't even feel all that tired, and Ryan, the store manager, had said Maggie could have Sunday off, no problem. Pressing the play button on the tape player while she pulled out of the parking lot, Maggie focused on the drive home. Alison Krauss's voice drifted out of the speakers, one of those sad and beautiful love songs.

Maggie and Ron both loved these songs. An intense sensation of sadness and longing brought tears to Maggie's eyes. Ron. Good, kind, decent Ron. Honest. Hardworking. A good dad, and a good husband. Maggie knew she would have missed his call tonight, but at least he would have talked to the kids.

Maggie entered the house as quietly as she could. Just as she had guessed, her mother and daughter were sleeping deeply on the couch. They often fell asleep watching TV. Maggie tiptoed to

Kenny's room. A strip of light shone at the top and bottom of the door. She knocked softly and then opened the door. Kenny was also asleep, his thin arm hanging over the edge of the bed, *Hoot* lying on the floor where it had fallen. Maggie walked softly to her son and watched his sleeping face. Kenny looked exactly like Ron, she thought. Slender, with dark brown hair and eyes that quickly showed black circles underneath when he was sick or tired or worried. Annette took after her, but Kenny was a carbon copy of his dad. Kenny had looked so stressed today when he left school, Maggie wondered if anything had happened. He wouldn't tell her. Ever since Kenny was a little boy – wasn't he *still* a little boy? – he hated delivering bad news.

"Kenny, honey, what happened to your arm?" Maggie had asked once at bath time, noticing a bruise on his forearm. Kenny was only five or so, an age when most children, like Annette, would have come howling for relief if only just for the attention.

"I think it was a bump on it, but it was just a little bump." Even then Kenny downplayed his own pain, more tuned in to his mother's. "It didn't hurt like a big bump."

Now Maggie stood and gazed quietly at her son, hoping this new kind of pain he was facing could be bearable – like a little bump. The bruise on his arm had faded, but what kind of lasting mark would this new pain leave? Kenny stirred and blinked.

"Hi, Mom," he smiled sleepily. "Dad called."

"Hi, sweetie," Maggie kissed his soft cheek and stoked his hair, sweaty against his forehead. "Good, I'm glad you got to talk to him. Ryan said I could have Sunday off."

Kenny's heart jumped. "That's good, huh?"

"Yeah, we'll get an early start. How was school?"

"Good." It was only a half-lie. School was always pretty good. Mrs. Juarez was a great teacher, and Kenny's easy-going personality kept things on an even keel. Maggie didn't want to pry. She knew she could trust Mrs. Juarez to let her know if there were ever any serious issues. She breathed a small sigh of relief as Kenny's eyes closed again.

"G'nite, sweetie," Maggie kissed him again.

"G'nite, Mom. I'm glad about Sunday."

"Me, too," Maggie whispered, careful to control the apprehension she felt. Kenny must be worried, too, she realized. Somehow they would be just fine. They had to be. Ron needed them to be.

Chapter 5 – Poetry Reading

Mrs. Juarez was buzzing with excitement. The Author's Chair was placed strategically at the front of the class. Everyone loved the Author's Chair. Even the shy kids who were hesitant to sit in it and read in front of classmates at the beginning of the school year had grown to eagerly anticipate an opportunity to share their work. This was due solely to Mrs. Juarez's encouragement and the fact that she herself read from the Author's Chair. Occasionally Mrs. Juarez even messed up, although the students suspected it was on purpose, to put everyone at ease. Mrs. Juarez encouraged students to correct her mistakes.

"You always learn from your mistakes, so never hesitate to point mine out!" Mrs. Juarez happily exclaimed. Students grew confident in her classroom. Mrs. Juarez set high expectations, and most importantly, she always provided the support students needed to be successful.

"Okay, I'll go first..." Mrs. Juarez sat in the Author's Chair and faced her audience. No reminder about being good listeners was necessary. They were well versed in this. Mrs. Juarez was always proud when a guest speaker visited. Of course, she, too, was a good listener. Across the hall Mrs. Mercer would grade papers or do crossword puzzles while guest speakers gave a talk on careers or some other presentation arranged by the principal. And there was no worry of Mrs. Mercer showing disrespect while her students read their original work in the Author's Chair since "Mrs. Misery" didn't have one, and students were never given the opportunity to read their work aloud. Mrs. Juarez's students were lucky, and they knew it.

"*The Sandwich...*" Mrs. Juarez began. "My brother made a sandwich, of jelly, eggs, and goo. Olives, ketchup, lettuce leaves, good ol' Elmer's glue. He topped it off with pumpernickel, bottomed it with rye. And when he took a bite of it, I thought that I would die!" Mrs. Juarez was thrilling the students with her own original poem. No creative assignment escaped her. Kenny laughed out loud, as did everyone else. There were a few wrinkled noses and groans as their teacher described her own "favorite food" in verse, a disgusting concoction created by her brother.

Kenny thought about his own poem. He had written about animal-shaped pancakes, comparing them to their little cousins – animal crackers. It was an especially good poem, Kenny thought, but when he woke up this morning he began to have second thoughts about reading it aloud in class. Mrs. Juarez always invited discussion about their writing, and now Kenny felt reluctant to set himself up for questions that might be awkward. Of course, Kenny was doing what was natural for him – imagining the worst.

"Hey, Kenny, why'd you write about animal pancakes?"

"Yeah, where did you get that idea?"

"Didn't you tell me that your dad make animal pancakes?"

"Yeah, I remember! Kenny's dad made animal pancakes. Is that why they're your favorite food?"

Kenny was eating cereal this morning when this imaginary scenario began to play itself out in his mind. Suddenly the poem he had worked so hard on and was so proud of seemed very, very wrong. Kenny could not subject himself to this kind of scrutiny. A gnawing feeling in his stomach made him lose his appetite. Breakfast sat untouched. His mom noticed his diminished appetite but didn't say anything. Kenny was so thin already.

Back in his room Kenny rooted around in the camouflage backpack. He removed the poem and put it on his desk. In a few minutes Mom would be driving him to school. Kenny had to think fast, and he did.

Now, remembering his quick thinking this morning, a greatly relieved Kenny focused on his classmates. Rachel Mason was going up to the Author's Chair. Kenny liked Rachel. She was always nice to everybody. He paid attention while she read her favorite food poem. It was about salsa that her uncle made. Kenny also liked Rachel's Uncle Erik. Uncle Erik had come into their class on Career Day and talked about being a pilot. Who would've guessed that a pilot could make salsa, too?

Rachel finished with a flourish, and everyone began singing her praises. It really was a good poem, and Rachel looked happy and embarrassed as she made her way to her seat. Mrs. Juarez was impressed, Kenny could tell. He wished he had his pancake poem, but it was too late. Really, no one would have interrogated him, and he knew it. But Kenny had panicked this morning. Besides, Mrs. Juarez would never allow students to make someone feel uncomfortable. Oh well. There was nothing Kenny could do about it now, and the poem he had scrawled off quickly this morning would have to do. Unfortunately, his backup poem was about ice cream – and so were half the poems that were being read.

After the poetry reading Mrs. Juarez explained the assignment. Students were to illustrate their favorite food on a white paper plate and to write their poem on the plate as well. This would be homework, and Mrs. Juarez planned to display the plates on the bulletin board, which was covered with a red and white checkered tablecloth and added the words: *Favorite Foods: Nutritious or Not?* It would look like a picnic table when it was finished. Kenny could just imagine it with all the ice cream pictures. And he was already pretty sure that ice cream was "not" nutritious.

"What a great bunch of authors I have in my class!" Mrs. Juarez announced. "You just never cease to amaze me! And I've learned something about you all today, too!"

"And we learned about you, *too!*" Some had asked Mrs. Juarez if they could copy her poem, and others asked if they were going to make a class book of the poems, which they often did with projects like this. It had been a great assignment, and everyone was in good spirits. Even Kenny no longer regretted swapping poems. Who knows? Maybe he had saved the day by doing so.

As Kenny solved word problems during math he again imagined what might have transpired and felt another surge of relief. If there was one thing Kenny avoided at all costs, it was discussing his dad in school. It had only been a month, and so far no one in class had mentioned it. Kenny liked to think no one knew, but deep inside he knew this couldn't be true.

Kenny tried to push the thoughts away. Concentration was becoming more difficult as tears kept filling his eyes. The letters in the word problems began to swim and blur together. *Troop 435 was holding a fundraiser. Holding, troops, raised, funds.* Tears spilled onto the pages of the math book. *Who cares about word problems*, Kenny thought. The ache in his heart was unbearable now. Who cares about favorite foods or poems or fundraisers or word problems or anything else when your dad is in prison?

C hapter 6 – The Nightmare

How had it happened? How could it be true? Even this morning when Kenny woke up he had momentarily forgotten, and then, like every single morning since his dad had been arrested it hit him in his stomach – hard, and sickeningly fast. Ron Evans was not a criminal. Kenny knew this. Kenny knew it instinctively, and yet, his dad had been taken from his family – arrested and convicted of a crime of which, Kenny was certain, his dad was innocent. It was that creep, Len Herd. Kenny seethed at the thought of the fly-by-night builder.

Nine months earlier Ron had quit his job at the fernery. Ron had worked there since high school and had been a foreman for over ten years. The owner, Clyde Newly, was the best boss in the world, or so Ron often remarked. But about a year ago, Clyde was killed in a car accident, and his son, Clyde, Jr. took over. Clyde, Sr. was barely cold in the ground when Junior began changing everything. Junior's harsh treatment of the workers shocked Ron and everyone else, but what could they do? The fern cutters were all Mexican immigrants, some undocumented, and they certainly weren't planning to report the abuse. The other ferneries were up in arms about it. The owners even approached Junior Newly, but to no avail.

Every night Ron and Maggie talked about it, but they didn't know what to do. Hector Rodriguez, one of Ron's best workers and closest friends at the fernery, confided that he, too, was looking for another job. Hector was a jack-of-all-trades, Ron always said, and the two men discussed their options. They would have liked to taken jobs at another fernery, but nothing was available.

Then one day it happened – both left the fernery and began working for Len Herd, the independent builder who had a questionable reputation around town, but who offered flexibility and opportunity. "It will hold us over 'til I find something better," Ron reassured Maggie. "I just can't take one more day of Junior. I'm telling you, he's going to be investigated and shut down. Things are bad." Maggie understood, and Ron, along with Hector, began working for Len Herd. Maggie worried.

"I've been told that Herd doesn't pay his bills." Maggie wanted to be supportive of her husband, but was worried about their welfare.

"I've heard even worse, but that's the way it is in a small town. There's always gossip. He just got the bid on a commercial property, so that's steady money for a while. It will give me time to find something better. I won't stay with him. It's just a stopgap. But I have to get out of that fernery."

And so it began. Len Herd would show up early in the morning having already picked up Hector, and the two would come inside for a cup of coffee before the three men left for the job site. Kenny remembered his parents' nervousness and didn't like the looks of Herd. Annette hid behind her mother when Len Herd gushed a phony sounding, "Good morning, there, little cutie!" Herd's reptilian eyes were narrow slits that darted furtively around the room. When he talked he did so with an air of authority that assumed all eyes and ears were standing by to absorb his self-perceived vast wisdom. Kenny instinctively disliked this man. *This guy's gotta be worse than Junior Newly*, thought Kenny, and wished Dad and Hector had stuck it out at the fernery. At least there Ron was foreman. Herd referred to Dad and Hector as "Flunky One, and Flunky Two... Ha! Ha! Just kidding!" Yeah. Right. Just kidding. What a jerk!

After about two months the routine was consistent. Len Herd and Hector Rodriguez would arrive in Herd's battered Ford Bronco about six-fifteen every morning, come into the Evans' home, and have a cup of coffee before the three departed for the job site. Herd became the instant expert on whatever topic came up – something that was mentioned on the morning news, or just a general topic of discussion. He was a real know-it-all, but Ron and Hector pretended not to notice.

"Didja see the car wash they're building out on the truck route? It'll never pass inspection," Herd reported knowingly, leaning back in the chair and sipping coffee. "That permit's gonna be pulled. I guarantee it."

"Hmmmm," Ron and Hector would nod, deferring to this new boss.

"I coulda bought that lot for fifty grand," Herd spoke in low tones as though he were conspiring to pass along state secrets. "They caught me between ex-wives, though, and I couldn't get my hands on the cash in time." Herd sneered when he said, "ex-wives" as though the wives were somehow responsible for Herd's ineptitude in business. Herd took another sip of coffee and looked around the kitchen as though he wanted to change the subject.

"Whatcha got there, sport?" Herd asked Kenny, who was packing up his math book into his camouflage backpack.

"Just math," Kenny replied, hurrying to end the conversation. He didn't like Len Herd's smooth confident sneer, the air of authority over Kenny's dad, over Hector, over everything.

"My best subject! If you ever need help, I'm your man!" Herd reached up as was his habit and nervously smoothed his coarse, greasy hair over his shining bald spot.

Criminy, thought Kenny, *as if I need this lame-o's help!*

They were building a small strip mall for someone from New Jersey. Apparently Len Herd had "a connection," as he called it. Kenny sometimes overheard Dad telling his mom about events of the day, and of course five mornings a week Kenny was subjected to Len Herd's version of events.

But now the strip mall sat uncompleted, a work-not-in-progress. And Kenny's dad was in a state prison, convicted of a crime he did not commit. How Kenny hated Len Herd! *He* was the cause of this nightmare.

C hapter 7 – Word Problems

Kenny forced himself back to the word problems. Sometimes schoolwork was the best thing he had going for him. A welcome distraction from the challenges his family faced, schoolwork provided a sense of normalcy in a world that had been tumultuously rocked. Mom had told Mrs. Juarez and the principal, Mr. Joseph. Neither treated Kenny any differently, and for that he was immeasurably grateful. Mrs. Juarez was always kind, and in a way Kenny felt that she was doing her best to look out for him. They'd had a conference one day after school. Kenny waited outside the classroom door while his mother explained the family's circumstances. When they called Kenny back in, he could see that both women had been crying, and Mr. Joseph wore a sad, tired expression. Mrs. Juarez put her hand on Kenny's shoulder.

"Kenny, you know I told the class on the first day of school that I am here for you if you need me — not just to teach you about reading and writing and math and science, but as someone who truly cares for you. Well, I need to remind you of that again. Kenny, I'm so sorry for your troubles," Mrs. Juarez stroked his head as she clutched his mother's hand, "for your family's troubles, and I want to help in any way I can. I believe there will be times when you feel very strong emotions — maybe very sad, or even angry — and that's okay." Mrs. Juarez choked back tears and continued.

"Any time — *any* time — you need to be alone or have quiet time, you may have it. You are a very responsible and trustworthy boy, and I know if you just need to go outside and walk around or go to the media center, or go to the office, it's okay."

Mr. Joseph nodded. "Feel free to come and talk to me anytime, Kenny." Mr. Joseph had been through this with other students. It did not get any easier with experience. Once he had found a student teacher crying in the faculty lounge after school.

"What's wrong?" Mr. Joseph inquired.

The student teacher's response was tentative.

"Cory. Van Nuys. I didn't know his dad was in jail. I told Cory to have his dad sign his homework, and…" but here she broke off and sobbed. Mr. Joseph had comforted her and reflected on this growing trend of students faced with incarceration in the family. The poor intern. College classes prepared her for writing lesson plans, planning field trips, and even classroom management, but she wasn't prepared for this. And now Kenny and Annette Evans' dad was in prison. What was happening in the world, Mr. Joseph wondered.

Kenny sighed and focused intently on his word problems. The way Mrs. Juarez taught word problems was so creative. Kenny couldn't believe every teacher didn't do it this way. Instead of hating them, everyone liked them, even kids who claimed to stink in math, like Kenny once did. He remembered the day Mrs. Juarez enlightened the class about word problems.

"Now, who just *loves* word problems?" A loud groan escaped from the fidgety fifth graders. Great… here comes the train leaving Cleveland, wherever that was, and the other train leaving somewhere else.

"I see," grinned Mrs. Juarez. "Well, let me put your minds at ease. From this day forward you really *are* going to love word problems." Mrs. Juarez definitely had their attention now. "Because," she continued, walking around the class, peering at the open math books, "every single math problem is already a word problem – the text book authors simply left out the words!"

"Huuuuuhhhhh?" a collective question mark escaped from twenty-plus fifth graders. Mrs. Juarez smiled broadly.

"Think about it. We talked at the beginning of the year about all of the symbols used in math. Math is simply a symbolic language – kind of a shorthand for telling a long story quickly. Read number seven, please..." she scanned the room, "...Kanesha."

Kanesha read the problem, "Four hundred and eight divided by twelve equals..."

"Great. Thank you, Kanesha. Now, what are the symbols in that problem? Dell?"

"The divide sign and the equals sign?" Dell answered the question with a question.

"That's right. Each sign is a symbol, just as we reviewed before. Are there any other symbols?" A thoughtful silence, and then one by one students began tentatively raising their hands. Others looked confused. There were only two symbols, after all. When about half of the students had raised their hands, Mrs. Juarez encouraged them. "Now – each of you tell someone who does *not* have his or her hand raised, just what you think the other symbols are."

There was an excited buzz of interaction around the room punctuated with "Huh?" and "Oh! I get it now!"

"Okay... besides the division and equals signs, what other symbols are there?" This time everyone was waving hard, hoping to be called on. "Kenny?" Kenny, who never thought he was good in math, suddenly felt someone had removed a dark curtain and exposed something new and exciting and wonderful.

"The numbers are symbols. The numbers mean something, too!"

"Absolutely!" gushed Mrs. Juarez. "Kenny, you're a great storyteller..." This was true. Kenny was generally recognized as one of the most creative writers in his class. "...Can you make up a story to go with these symbols?" Kenny thought. Everyone was silent. Each was working up a story just in case Kenny couldn't come up with something. Mrs. Juarez waited and smiled encouragingly.

"Uh... there were 408 books donated to our school by the PTA. Since there are two classes each, from kindergarten through fifth grade, that makes a total of 12 classes. So, how many books will each class receive if they're divided up equally?" Kenny ended on a note of confidence. He was sure this is what Mrs. Juarez had in mind. She smiled broadly and spoke excitedly.

"Perfect! Absolutely perfect! Now I owe you twenty dollars!" Everyone laughed. Mrs. Juarez often said that when someone gave the most perfect answer as Kenny had clearly done. "I could not have come up with a better story myself!" she exclaimed. "Now, let's divide up these problems, and each of you will have the opportunity to come up with a fun story to go with the 'symbols' in your math problem."

From that day forward Kenny, and everyone else, for that matter, had developed a whole new appreciation for word problems, and in fact, a whole new appreciation for their teacher. They would never be intimidated by a word problem again. To think, it was just that simple. All you had to do was go backwards! Math really was a symbolic language, and Kenny's gift for storytelling was put to good use.

As he finished the assignment, Officer Randall, the D.A.R.E. officer entered smiling. Kenny took a deep breath. Great! Just when he was having a pretty good day! Gripping his pencil and squaring his jaw, Kenny looked determinedly ahead. Kenny was *not* going to let this get to him.

Chapter 8 – Teachers are Superheroes

The D.A.R.E. officer was popular with all of the students, even Kenny. Kenny knew it was the sight of the uniform that triggered the emotional reaction yesterday, conjuring up the image of his dad being arrested. Kenny's thinness shrunk even smaller. He wished he could disappear. Sitting rigidly, his pain-filled eyes looked beseechingly towards his teacher. Mrs. Juarez wore a half-shocked, half-horrified look on her face. Mrs. Juarez knew, of course, that Officer Randall's presence would be uncomfortable for Kenny, but she was more concerned with the topic – drugs. What could be done? How could one teacher save the day?

One other time in her teaching career Mrs. Juarez was faced with a painfully awkward situation similar to this. A representative of the Boy Scouts had come to the class to extend an invitation. "I'm sorry, girls," the scout leader said as he handed out brochures to the boys, "this will just be a minute that I have to talk to the gentlemen. Just ignore me, ladies." As the scout master launched into his talk, he suddenly noticed Donna Pelkey in the front row. Donna had short hair and was dressed in blue jeans and a T-shirt. "Oh, here, sorry I missed you…" he apologized, handing Donna a recruitment brochure. Donna's horrified expression told all. Donna's eyes met Mrs. Juarez's, her mouth gaped, and she pushed the brochure to the floor and put her head down on her desk, too mortified to speak. The Boy Scout leader was aghast. "I'm so sorry…" he whispered to Mrs. Juarez, who simply froze as the scout master half-heartedly finished his talk and quickly left.

Mrs. Juarez never forgave herself for not saving Donna. But even all these years later, she still wasn't sure how she could have spared her that particular embarrassment. Now it felt like she was reliving that same event, only the stakes were greater, perhaps. *Quick*, she thought, *do something!*

"Oh, Officer Randall! I am so, so sorry," Mrs. Juarez began. "I completely forgot you were scheduled to speak today, and I went and scheduled a very important test review," Mrs. Juarez lied. "Boys and girls, I'm sorry. I know you were counting on Officer Randall's activity, and I feel just terrible that I didn't double check my schedule!" The students were nonplussed. Sure, they liked the D.A.R.E. officer's visits, but whatever. "Please get into teams for Numbered Heads Together so we can begin our review."

Mrs. Juarez had taken Officer Randall by the elbow and was escorting him out the door. Stepping outside with him, she partially closed the door, whispered, "Sorry! I'll explain later!" and returned to her class. Mrs. Juarez had known Pat Randall for years. She would call him later to explain. Pat would understand.

What an afternoon! There were two very relieved people when school ended that day – Kenny and Mrs. Juarez. Kenny lingered a few minutes longer than usual. He needed to thank Mrs. Juarez. Kenny wanted her to know that he saw what she did, and he was grateful. He didn't want her thinking that he took her kindness for granted. This was the first time Kenny had spoken with her since his mom had the conference. She seemed to be expecting him and smiled warmly.

"Mrs. Juarez," Kenny began, "thanks for canceling D.A.R.E. today." He hesitated. "I… uh, I know it was for me." Kenny didn't cry, but faced her stoically and gratefully, clutching his backpack tightly.

"It's okay…" now she hesitated. "It caught me off guard."

They both were silent for a moment, pondering the inevitable but unspoken question. What about the next time, and the time after that? She just couldn't go on canceling the D.A.R.E. officer indefinitely. But both had had enough stress for one day.

"Don't worry," Mrs. Juarez reassured him. "We'll figure this out. It will be fine."

Kenny believed her. This teacher would find a resolution.

"How's your dad doing?" Mrs. Juarez almost hated to ask, but felt that the moment was right.

"Good. He called last night and I talked to him. We're going to see him on Sunday. My mom got off work." Kenny blurted everything out in a hurry, eager to get it off his chest and make it real. He really missed his dad and hadn't seen him since he was sentenced.

"I'm glad, Kenny," Mrs. Juarez spoke gently. "I'm sure he misses you very much, so I'm glad you're going to see him." She really didn't know what else to say. In all her years of teaching Mrs. Juarez had known of students whose father, and once even a mother, had been incarcerated, but this was the first time it had occurred during the school year. So in years past they were students who were already used to dealing with it, or at least the shock had worn off. It made her sad to watch Kenny fidget or daydream, clearly upset and distracted, and he would never know the tears she cried on his behalf. Kenny was such a forlorn looking thing, she thought, especially with those big dark circles under his beautiful brown eyes. Kids sure had it hard sometimes. *They are all at the mercy of the adults in their world*, Mrs. Juarez thought. *And what a sad reality that is.*

Chapter 9 – Is Daddy Bad?

Kenny hurried to the student pick-up area where his mom and Annette would be waiting in their old minivan. As he hurried down the sidewalk, Gabe DeJoy, Kenny's best friend since third grade caught up with him. Gabe was in Mrs. Mercer's class this year, and the boys had been in different classes in fourth grade, too. But the two remained close friends and usually played together at recess.

"Hey! Did you guys get the ball pumped back up?"

"Yeah, but it's got a leak, so Mrs. Juarez said she'd see about patching it or getting a new one." The fifth graders either played kickball or watched the others playing kickball at recess each day. On Fridays Mrs. Juarez played spelling kickball with them. She'd roll the ball, call out the spelling word, and the kicker had to spell the word correctly in order to kick and run the bases.

"Dang." Gabe always said 'dang.' "I hope she fixes it by tomorrow. Hey! Did you find out if you can come yet?" Gabe had invited Kenny and some of the other guys to his birthday party this Sunday. It was going to be a blast. Gabe's dad was taking them all to the rock climbing gym and having a pizza party. It would be cool. Kenny hadn't forgotten about the party. In fact, he had looked forward to accepting the invitation but had to wait to find out if his mom could get off work. Since Maggie had, Kenny's plans took a new direction.

"I wish I could," Kenny told Gabe. "But I can't. Not this Sunday."

"Dang! It's gonna be so much fun! They teach you how to climb, like twenty or thirty feet straight up. It's like mountain climbing."

"I know," Kenny sighed, happy to have reached the van. "But I can't," he repeated, opening the door to climb in.

"Hi, Gabe! How are you?"

"Hi, Mrs. Evans," Gabe returned the greeting. "Fine. Can Kenny come to my party on Sunday? It's not dangerous." Gabe had heard all the arguments already from other mothers.

"Not this Sunday. We have plans, I'm afraid," Maggie said, glancing at Kenny who apparently hadn't told Gabe where he was going. "Maybe we can plan something special for you two later," she offered.

"Okay," Gabe reluctantly agreed as he waved and headed down the sidewalk. He threw his hand up in a wave. "See ya, Kenny!"

"See ya!"

"How was your day?" Maggie Evans asked. Annette hadn't arrived yet, and it gave Maggie a chance to speak to Kenny by himself. She was looking carefully at him now, knowing he had to be disappointed at missing Gabe's birthday party. Maggie feared that Kenny might resent having to spend the day visiting Ron in prison. Lately he seemed testy over the smallest things.

"Okay," Kenny reassured her, sensing her concern. "It's okay about Gabe's party. I'd rather go and see Dad. I told Mrs. Juarez we were going. She asked how he was." He blurted out everything. "She cancelled the D.A.R.E. officer today, too. It kind of freaked us both out, I think, when Officer Randall came in. But I know we have to have the D.A.R.E. program."

Wow. This was a lot of information, thought Maggie. She could see that although Kenny was tested by the events of the day, he seemed somewhat stronger, more confident, at having survived them. And having Mrs. Juarez's support and kindness certainly made a difference. Maybe this adjustment would not take too great a toll on their children, Maggie silently hoped.

Just then a wailing Annette rounded the corner, Mrs. Morton holding her hand, bent over and comforting her as she led Annette to the minivan. Maggie and Kenny both jumped out in concern. Mrs. Morton's presence alerted them that this was not a simple case of Annette whining for her own way, and both mother and brother looked for physical signs of Annette's distress. Annette sobbed as Maggie scooped her up and kissed the top of her curly head, Annette's wet face pressed against her mother's neck.

"Mrs. Evans, I'm so sorry," began Mrs. Morton. "Another student was teasing Annette," she hesitated, lowered her voice and mouthed the words, "about your husband. Being, uh, *in prison...*" The last two words were barely audible, but Kenny and Maggie both cringed upon hearing them. Poor Annette! Who had done this? Kenny wanted to smack whoever it was!

"I had a serious talk with the student, and I've called her mother about it," Mrs. Morton continued. *Oh, no*, Kenny thought, *it was going to be all over school now about his dad being in prison!*

"Mommy, Kelsey said Daddy is *bad*!" sobbed Annette, more angry than hurt. Kelsey was just a first-grader. Kenny couldn't smack her.

"It's okay, baby," Maggie reassured her. "She was mixed up. She didn't mean it."

"I'm sorry," Mrs. Morton continued. "I won't allow teasing like that, you can be sure." Kenny realized then that his mother had to have had a talk with Annette's teacher, too. The sudden realization that *every* teacher knew about his dad made him flush with shame. *I hate Len Herd*, thought Kenny. *I hate him and hope he dies.*

"Thank you, Mrs. Morton," Maggie whispered, saddened at this news. Maggie was not surprised and knew her children would face challenges like this. A few students stared as they trudged by on the way to the waiting buses and cars, but none seemed too interested in a crying first-grader. It was not the most unusual sight in the world, after all. "Thanks for taking care of it," Maggie repeated. "Annette will be okay."

Mrs. Morton looked troubled as she patted Annette's head and then Mrs. Evans' arm. She opened her mouth to say something, and then awkwardly closed it, nodded and walked away. The Evans family got into their minivan. Annette had stopped crying, and allowed her mother to buckle her seatbelt without the usual resistance. No one spoke as Maggie started the van and pulled out. Kenny's stomach was tied up in knots.

After a few miles, Mrs. Evans asked Annette if she was feeling better. Annette was not typically a quiet child. Annette simply nodded her head and didn't say anything.

"Honey, I'm sorry about what Kelsey said," Maggie tried. "Remember we talked about this before?" Maggie fumbled for words. "Kelsey didn't mean it," Maggie said halfheartedly.

"Is Daddy bad?" Annette asked softly, as though she were afraid it might be true.

Before Maggie had a chance to respond she was startled by the swift and heated outburst from her son.

"*No!* Dad is *not* bad! He didn't do anything wrong except work for a jerk who is evil and rotten and caused *all* of this!" Kenny ranted. Trembling with rage, he continued. "He's the best dad in the world, Annette. *You* know that! He didn't do anything. He shouldn't be in prison. It's *all wrong!*" And then Kenny, too burst into tears. Maggie Evans pulled the minivan into a parking lot and shut off the engine, unbuckling her seat belt all in one motion. She reached over and held her sobbing son, his thin shoulders heaving, head pressed against her. Suddenly Kenny pulled away, opened the door and began to throw up.

Annette began to cry again. Maggie was frantic. She had to get them both calmed down. "It's okay, it's okay," Maggie's voice soothed as she jumped out and held Kenny. She found some leftover napkins in the console and wiped his face. "Come on, honey, calm down... It's okay... Annette, come here, honey..." Maggie held her two children tightly, stroking their heads and whispering reassuringly, "There, there... it's going to be okay." Maggie's own tears would come later, in private. First she must soothe her children.

Hours later, when the hysterics had finally subsided, the Evans family evening routine was quieter than usual. Maggie found Kenny sound asleep in the recliner, the dark circles under his eyes deeper than usual. As Annette often did, she had escaped in a TV show and was looking worn out, too. Maggie stared at her two children and wondered how the three of them were going to get through this.

Maggie tiptoed into the little computer room to check her email. There was the usual junk mail and a message from her sister, Amy. Thank goodness for family. If only Amy lived closer. But at least she had her mom close by. That was something. Maggie clicked on Amy's message. The subject line read: *Legal help for Ron?*

Hi Mag – I was surfing the net and found this site. Do you think it could help?

Maggie clicked on the link to writeaprisoner.com, curious as to what Amy was suggesting. As Maggie surfed the site she realized that it was comprised mainly of inmates from prisons everywhere who were looking for pen pals. *Ron doesn't need pen pals, he has us*, Maggie thought. Then she saw the link Amy must have been suggesting – for legal assistance. *This might help*, Maggie dared to hope. Ron intended to appeal the conviction. Maggie believed he was innocent, and with the right legal help she and Ron believed that the conviction could be overturned. How she hated Len Herd! Kenny was right. Len Herd was an evil person and solely responsible for the family's trouble. Maggie hated that her children were tainted by all of this, but she especially hated that her husband, a good and honest person was languishing this very minute in a cramped prison cell, his good name and reputation sullied, his family humiliated and desperately missing him.

Maggie continued to surf the site. She found herself reading postings on the chat forum written by friends and family members of inmates. *So many people are in prison*, Maggie realized. She never thought much about people in prison until Ron's situation. Now Maggie was acutely aware each time she read new statistics in the paper. Her sister, Amy, researched everything online and often forwarded news stories to her about stories similar to Ron's. Maggie clicked on a posting by someone who called herself "Delaware Princess" titled "PP beaten up."

Help! Hadn't heard from my PP so I contacted his institution in TX. He's in the infirmary, got beat up, so I called his grandmother and only relative there in TX but she didn't know anything about it!!!!! Doesn't the prison notify family? What kind of deal is this???!!!

Maggie figured out that 'PP' was pen pal, and as she read the responses to Delaware Princess's question she felt mixed emotions. What if Ron gets beat up in prison? Would someone call her? Apparently not. And what else might happen to him there? Maggie tried not to dwell on this as she read the dozen or so responses. What she sensed most of all was the community of support that these pen pals of prisoners provided to each other. Some were family members, some were simply voluntary pen pals, but all were sensitive to each other's feelings regarding the plight of the inmates.

Maggie sighed and logged off. She wasn't sure if the legal posting was a good idea, but she would talk to Ron about it and Amy, too. Amy could always think clearly and give good advice. She probably ought to forward the information to Leticia, too, Hector's wife. Right now, though, Maggie needed to look after her children.

C hapter 10 – The Long Drive

Kenny yawned and readjusted his seatbelt. His mom had awakened him so early that it was technically still night out. She had barely touched his shoulder and his eyes flew wide open. Through his window Kenny saw the moon in the dark sky, like a bright flashlight shining towards their house.

"Time to get up, Kenny," his mom spoke softly. Kenny had jumped out of bed and dressed swiftly, a sense of urgency about him. Now he was silent as his mom drove the back roads heading out toward the interstate. There was no traffic.

Annette had fallen back asleep, her head leaning against the window in the back seat. Kenny was excited, but his emotions were jumbled up inside him. He couldn't wait to see his dad. How he missed him! But he was also afraid. Afraid of the prison and what it would be like. Afraid of the guards and the other prisoners. He was simply afraid of so many unknowns.

Kenny looked over at his mom. She was hunched over the steering wheel, gripping it tightly, eyes straight ahead. She looked tired. Not tired like when you first wake up, Kenny thought, but tired from carrying a heavy burden a long time. It had begun to rain, and she turned on the wipers.

Slap – whoosh, slap – whoosh, slap – whoosh…

On the passenger side the wiper blade needed to be replaced. It had needed to be replaced for a long time, and Maggie always said she meant to do it, but then it would stop raining and she would forget. Kenny remembered – it was only a few months ago – his dad intending to replace the blade for Maggie.

"I picked up new blades at the auto parts store," he had told her. "Help me remember to do it this weekend." But he forgot, and so did she, and then the nightmare began. Kenny wished he knew how to do it. It probably wasn't that hard. Filling in for his dad was going to be serious business, he realized. What if he had to get a job, too? He knew that Leticia Hernandez had started cleaning houses to earn extra money, and he didn't want his mom to have to do that. She already worked at Publix, and she was grateful that she usually only had to work the day shift.

Slap – whoosh, slap – whoosh, slap – whoosh…

The windshield wipers were hypnotic. Kenny's bleary eyes felt heavy, but he didn't want to sleep. The clock on their dashboard didn't work, so he had no idea what time it was. But if his mom had to stay awake to drive, he should try to stay awake with her.

"Too bad it's raining," he said. She smiled and shook her head a little.

"Yeah… but it's okay since there's no traffic to speak of. I'm watching for deer, though. Remember all those deer we saw that time coming back from Alabama? That's all we need, for a deer to jump out." Maggie kept her eyes on the road and gave Kenny a quick smile.

"I'll watch, too," he volunteered.

"When we get on the interstate we'll drive through McDonald's for breakfast," she promised. "There's nothing open yet. Heck, it's the middle of the night, practically! I could sure use a Diet Coke." Maggie yawned. "Maybe we'll find a convenience store that's open. I forgot to pick some up yesterday."

"Okay," Kenny replied as he watched for deer and tried to keep his eyes awake. He could use a cold drink, too. He would watch for convenience stores now, too.

Suddenly he opened his eyes with a jerk. It was daylight! He had fallen asleep. Kenny looked guiltily over at his mom who smiled at him. "It's okay," Maggie reassured him, "you were tuckered out." Kenny hated that he had let his mom down. He was supposed to be watching for deer and a convenience store. He realized they were on the interstate. He must have been sleeping for hours.

"Sorry I fell asleep," he yawned. At least the rain had stopped.

"There's a McDonald's at the next exit," Maggie said. "Are you hungry?"

"Kind of," Kenny replied, looking out the window. He felt stiff and wanted to get out and walk around to wake up. He was mad at himself for falling asleep. Annette stirred in the back seat.

"Mommy, I have to go to the bathroom," she announced.

"Good morning, sweetie," Maggie smiled into the rearview mirror at Annette, "We're almost to McDonald's, okay?" Annette's face lit up.

"Can I get pancakes?" she asked. Oh, great, thought Kenny. She'll make a sticky mess out of things if she has pancakes in the car. And then, as if she were reading his mind she promised, "I'll be careful."

Maggie smiled again. "Sure can! In fact, I think we'll just sit down and have breakfast inside. We're doing good on time."

Thirty minutes later the minivan pulled back onto the interstate highway. Kenny wondered how much longer it would be. The night before he overheard his mom on the phone. Maggie was telling Leticia Hernandez that it would take about four hours to drive to the prison. Hector was in a different prison, but apparently it wasn't too far from the one where Ron Evans was incarcerated. The two women often discussed their situation on the phone, and Kenny knew his mom would plan the drive so the family could have the full amount of visitation time with Dad.

Kenny thought about Gabe's birthday party today. Oh well. He knew his mom would do something to make it up to him. He had dropped Gabe's gift off yesterday – a new video game. Kenny saw Maggie talking to Gabe's mom in the kitchen. *I guess everyone does know about Dad,* he had thought. But Kenny hadn't mentioned his dad to Gabe when he gave him the birthday gift. Kenny wondered if the other kids would talk about it, about him, during the party. His absence would certainly be noted, of that he was certain. Kenny pushed the image of his friends discussing his dad in prison out of his mind. What was the use in worrying? Kenny felt himself grow angry inside. If any of the kids ever said anything about his dad he would let them have it! Even Gabe!

Kenny sighed. Maggie noticed his deep concentration and felt the apprehension grow inside of her. She had been to see Ron at the county facility when he was waiting to be sentenced, but this was the first trip to the state prison. It had taken this long to complete all of the necessary paperwork for an approved visit. Maggie had some idea of what to expect because she had filled out the forms and read the guidelines, but she couldn't be entirely sure. And the kids. She didn't know how they would react to seeing Ron in this way. Maggie worried more about Kenny than Annette.

"Well, we're almost there," Maggie finally said. She had been referring to her Mapquest printout during the drive and began slowing down for the exit. Everyone was silent, watching out the window, not sure exactly what they were looking for.

Blink-uh, blink-uh, blink-uh…

The turn signal was the only sound as they waited for an old blue car to pass by. All eyes peered forward as Maggie pulled out. They drove silently for another mile or so. Time seemed to have slowed down. Then they saw the sign: State Correctional Institution – 1 Mile Ahead. Kenny was numb. He did not feel nervous or afraid or even excited at the thought of seeing his dad. He felt completely numb.

As they came around the bend it appeared suddenly. A large, nondescript brick building surrounded by walls topped with three rows of curled barbed wire. A guard tower loomed over the structure. It was indeed an institution and as impersonal as any factory might have been. The reddish color of the bricks made Kenny think of a school. For one split second Kenny thought that maybe his dad was going to school. Maggie pulled into the parking lot where the old blue car that had passed by them back at the exit was parking. She pulled the van in alongside the car. All three watched as an elderly woman about Gram's age get out. She was taking her car key off of her key ring. As the Evans family exited the van, Maggie spoke a tentative "Good morning" to the woman.

"Good morning," the woman smiled back. "First time here?" It must have shown on their faces. Maggie nodded. "You can only take your ignition key in with you," the woman advised. "Otherwise they'll make you bring them back out anyway." Maggie was visibly shaken. She thought she had read all the rules carefully ahead of time. How had she missed that?

"And," the woman continued, "you'll need ones and change for the vending machines. The guards can't give you change." Maggie nodded. She knew this. Ron had told her. The money had to be carried in a see-through change purse or plastic sandwich bag.

"Thank you," Maggie spoke softly, placing her key ring on the console and locking up the van. Together the four of them strode purposefully toward the prison entrance. Kenny felt light-headed but said nothing. He tried to make himself feel numb again. Thank goodness the old woman kept the conversation going and distracted them.

"How far of a drive did you have?" she asked.

"Just around four hours," Maggie answered as they walked up the steps. "How about you?"

"Six. But I'm used to it now." The woman looked resigned. Her smallish shoulders sagged under a baggy sweatshirt.

They stood outside the big glass doors. Maggie seemed distracted, hesitant, and the old woman opened the door. Kenny quickly went forward and took the door, holding it for everyone.

When he stepped inside he was awestruck at the sight of the place. Empty, stark, and sterile. The polished floor shone under the harsh fluorescent lighting. Something that resembled the metal detectors at the airport stood to the left. Warning signs and policy statements plastered a long counter that loomed large in the center of the room. And two uniformed guards sat behind the counter, just staring at the newly arrived visitors.

Chapter 11 – Getting In

The old lady led the way to the counter where visitors signed in and got clearance to go into the visiting room. She seemed to be silently reassuring Maggie: *Don't worry. Watch what I do. It's not hard.*

"How ya doin' this mornin', Mizz Curtis?" the younger guard asked the woman. His familiarity with her reassured Kenny somehow.

"Good. Good. How 'bout you?"

"Ah, just fine," he replied handing her a clipboard. "How was the drive up?"

"Not too bad except for some rain," she responded, chatting about the weather as she provided the requested information.

"Here you go," the woman said to Maggie, handing her the clipboard. Maggie took it and followed the woman's lead.

"Name of inmate?" the other guard was asking Maggie.

"Huh?" She was startled as he spoke directly to her for the first time. "Oh. Uh. Ron. Uh, Ronald Evans."

Name of inmate, thought Kenny. His dad was an inmate. A prisoner. He felt shame and humiliation standing there while his mom signed them in and showed her ID. Kenny watched the younger guard who was courteous, even friendly. The phone rang often. Kenny didn't understand the snippets of conversation. Uniformed personnel came and went, the guards buzzing them in and out of small, windowed rooms with electronic locks. It reminded Kenny of a sci-fi movie.

"Step behind the white line for your photo," the older guard commanded Maggie. There was no inflection in his voice, no emotion at all. Maggie looked to where the guard was pointing.

"Right there," whispered Mrs. Curtis, who by now had taken them all under her wing and was helping them feel more comfortable.

Maggie stepped over and looked up at a wall-mounted camera.

"Thank you," the guard said. "All done." He was all efficiency.

Maggie gathered Kenny and Annette close to her and spoke to Mrs. Curtis.

"Thank you for all your help," she spoke sincerely and quietly. "This is a bit nerve wracking."

"Believe me, I understand. My son's in his fifth year, and I'm finally adjusted. Sort of. It's never easy."

The two women spoke and waited. The front doors opened and three more people entered. Three young women, one with a baby on her hip. They were laughing and joking.

"We're baaaaaaaaaack!" the first one called to the young guard.

"Here's trouble," he joked. He grinned at the young woman. She was heavyset with bright red hair and wore lots of makeup and jewelry. She looked like she was going to a party instead of to a prison, Kenny observed. Clearly the leader of the group, she swaggered toward the desk. "You're late!" the younger guard chastised in a good-natured way.

"Hah! You haven't let anybody in yet, I'll bet," she retorted. Kenny was amazed. He couldn't believe this woman would banter with the guard in such a bold way. But she did, grinning all the while. As the three women went through the routine of signing in, Kenny, Annette, Mom, and Mrs. Curtis were told to go through the metal detector and on through to the next phase of visitation. This included having their hands stamped with some kind of invisible ink. The older guard stamped them and didn't speak. Again, Maggie followed Mrs. Curtis' lead.

"They use a special light to see if your hand's stamped when you come and go," she explained to Maggie.

Kenny was fascinated by the invisible ink. So was Annette who kept trying to see what was stamped on her hand.

"I can't see what it is," Annette complained. The guard held up the stamp so she could see it.

"A teddy bear," he said. Sure enough, it was a cute little teddy bear, the very kind of stamp a first grade teacher like Mrs. Morton might use to stamp the students' hands with. Go figure, thought Kenny. The prison has a teddy bear stamp. These inconsistent images – teddy bears and joking guards – confused him. When he thought of a prison he thought of the other aspects – the barbed wire, locks, and cells. He wondered what the cells were like. He had seen enough TV and movies to imagine, but he wondered what it was *really* like.

Beeeeeeeeeeeeeeeep! The girl with the baby set off the metal detector. Everyone jumped.

"She's trying to smuggle something!" the redhead laughed. Embarrassed, the young mother went back and removed her shoes. This time she came through without beeping.

"Shut up!" she cautioned the redhead. "You'll get me in trouble!"

"Nah, you'll get yourself in trouble, smuggling in those Pampers!" the young guard laughed. The young woman did have a handful of disposable diapers. Kenny suddenly realized it must be hard to bring young children into the prison. He remembered when Annette was a baby, his mother never went anywhere without a well-stocked diaper bag. This young mother was allowed to carry the diapers but nothing else. Prisons were very strict places.

The redhead teased again. "Just throw her man in the hole. It'll do him good." Kenny believed he knew what "the hole" was and couldn't believe how this girl so brazenly joked about such things. But she did, and the other two young women just laughed along with the young guard. The older guard just looked bored as he motioned everyone to approach a big glass door. Suddenly there was a very loud, sustained, *"Errrrrrrrrrr!"* It was the sound of the electronic lock. The young guard swung the door open and held it for the eight visitors. Kenny looked around and realized that besides the guard, he was the only male. This was it. They were going inside the prison.

Kenny stayed close to his mom, who stayed close to Mrs. Curtis. Everyone was silent now, even the joking girls. They all followed the guard through a courtyard area to another big glass door and heard the same startling sound as someone from inside unlocked it. Again, the guard held the door.

Following Mrs. Curtis, each person stepped up to a window where another guard viewed their hands held under an ultraviolet light. Now Annette could see the teddy bear on her hand – the innocuous teddy bear stamp that in the outside world might mean, "Good job!" but here in the prison world meant, "Not an inmate!"

In a few minutes they were standing at a desk in the visiting room. The guard seated there scanned the vacant room and eyed the visitors. He looked at the names listed on his computer monitor and scanned again. Kenny and Annette were busy looking around the room. Snack machines stood against one wall, and there were rows of plastic chairs bolted to the floor.

"Curtis. Back corner," the guard pointed. Mrs. Curtis mumbled a thank you and went to seat herself in the space he had indicated.

"Evans. Over there…" he nodded to another corner. Maggie led Kenny and Annette by their hands. Kenny usually didn't hold hands with his mom, but it felt reassuring right now. The guard continued to seat the visitors, all spaced apart from each other. In one way, it reminded Kenny of being seated in a restaurant, but in another sense, his intuition told him it had something to do with security issues. He doubted very much that anyone here cared whether the visitors and inmates had any privacy for their conversations.

As soon as they were seated Annette wanted to get something out of the vending machines.

"I'm still hungry," she claimed.

"Wait until Daddy comes out. Then we can get him something, too," Maggie hushed her. Kenny could see that his mom was very nervous. His heart ached for her. His gaze took in the room. Mrs. Curtis caught his eye and smiled at him. Kenny smiled back and reflected on their luck at meeting her in the parking lot. In the ceiling there were lots of camera bubbles. Kenny knew what these were. His dad had shown him the hidden cameras at Wal-Mart one time. He guessed this was so guards could keep an eye on everyone. The three young women were seated nearer to each other. They were still conversing, the redhead clearly the dominant personality. Kenny was glad for the distraction they had provided so far this morning.

Where was his dad? Where were the other inmates? As Kenny scanned the room he took in all the details. A small play area for children contained a few toys. There were restrooms, the doors marked with large letters, "VISITORS ONLY!" Through the window Kenny could see the courtyard they had passed through from the reception area. He thought of his dad looking out of this window, freedom just a few feet away, but denied to him. Tears welled up in his eyes. *I can't cry*, he thought. *I can't cry here.*

"Mommy, where's Daddy?" Annette was eager to explore the vending machines.

"He'll be here in a minute, honey," Maggie spoke softly. "Just be patient. Daddy's going to be so happy to see his girl!" She squeezed Annette close to her.

Suddenly a door Kenny hadn't noticed swung open. He heard the jangle of keys and saw another guard come in. Behind him was a young man wearing a brownish-burgundy shirt and pants, followed by others dressed the same way. Prisoners! They were coming in. Kenny was spellbound. The prisoners were ushered up to the desk where they were checked in. The redhead rushed up to the desk.

"Baby! Baby!" she cooed, hugging and kissing the first prisoner. He was tall and tattooed, his hair cut so short it was almost shaved. He hugged her hard and kissed her harder. It reminded Kenny of how they kissed in the movies.

Mrs. Curtis had hurried to the desk when the men were brought in. Kenny tried to guess which one was her son, but it was no challenge since they were beaming at each other. Mother and son hugged and greeted each other warmly before going to their assigned corner to sit and visit.

Maggie, Annette, and Kenny were fascinated. The reunions between the inmates and visitors were touching. Bittersweet. Sad. But where was Ron? Kenny began to worry. He could see his mom was worried, too. A new group of visitors had arrived. Two more young women and an older woman who led a girl about Kenny's age by the hand. The desk guard directed them to their seats. Kenny watched as the girl and the older woman came to sit on the row behind the Evans family.

"Hi," the woman smiled at Maggie.

"Hi," Maggie nervously replied.

"Mom, I'm going to get something to eat," the girl announced, almost defiantly.

"Fine," her mother sighed as she seated herself in one of the plastic chairs. Kenny stared as the girl flounced over to the vending machines, opened a clear plastic bag full of quarters, and began buying snacks. *Maybe they didn't stop for breakfast,* he thought. The girl, tall, with short, curly brown hair pulled back by barrettes, wearing jeans, sneakers, and a pink sweatshirt that had a crown and "Princess" printed across it, deposited quarter after quarter, pressed button after button, and filled her arms with chips, sandwiches, donuts, candy, and soda. She strode back to where her mother was seated and dumped the load of food onto an empty seat.

"There!" the girl announced. "They're out of those chicken salad sandwiches he likes," she complained. Kenny wondered about the girl, although he knew it was impolite to stare and eavesdrop, as he was clearly doing. Besides, he was here to see his dad. Where *was* he?

Kenny looked back over at the door the guards used to bring in the inmates. He looked at his mom and wondered how long they had been waiting. A gnawing feeling began in his stomach. Something had gone wrong. Kenny looked at his mom. Maggie continued in her distracting chit-chat with Annette, and Kenny realized it was as much for his mom's diversion as for Annette's.

Suddenly the door swung open. The jangling keys announced the arrival of more inmates. And there, looking much older than Kenny remembered stood his dad.

C hapter 12 – The Visit

"Daddy! Daddy! Daddy!" Annette lunged for her dad as Maggie quickly scooped her daughter up with one arm and smoothed her own hair back with her free hand. Maggie smiled tentatively at Ron as she headed for the desk where Ron would be cleared to join his family. In a blur of time and motion the family suddenly converged into hugs and kisses and choruses of "How are you?"

"Kenny! You look taller! How are you? Annette! How's my girl? Maggie!" Ron was so happy. It had been so long, and talking on the phone just wasn't sufficient. Oh, to hold them close like this was wonderful! Annette sat on his lap and made her request.

"Daddy? Can I get something out of the machines?" She pointed toward the vending machines and eyed the contents. "I'm hungry."

Maggie and Ron smiled at each other. Annette was always hungry. Some things never changed, and this small reality was somehow reassuring.

"Sure, honey, what are you hungry for?" Ron snuggled his daughter as she gazed longingly toward the vending machines.

"I don't know," Annette's voice trailed off as she looked at the loot the girl behind them had purchased. Suddenly she spun back around and asked, "Daddy! Are you coming home today?"

Ron hung his head and reached out for her. "No, not today, but soon, Annette... I'll come home soon." And then, changing the subject, "I liked the picture you sent me with your name going both directions! I hung it up in my ce... uh.... in my room," Ron faltered. His gaze met Maggie's. Both looked so sad. Kenny was feeling that numb feeling again. Suddenly he swung into action.

"Annette! Let's see if they have Skittles!" He jumped up and grabbed the Ziploc bag full of one dollar bills and quarters. "Can we, Mom?"

"That's a great idea. Annette, you can get Daddy a snack."

"Okay!" Annette charged towards the machine that held potato chips and candy bars. Ron smiled, mesmerized at her bouncing curls. Inmates were not allowed to handle the money or go the machines. Annette would gladly spend the day taking orders and going back and forth to make purchases. Kenny knew this, and he instinctively knew his mom and dad would probably like some private time to talk. He joined Annette at the vending machines and stole one little glance over his shoulder at his parents. They weren't talking, just locked in a tight embrace. Kenny turned his focus back to Annette. She had already made her first selection.

"How much is Skittles?"

"Sixty-five cents." Kenny slid a dollar into the machine and showed Annette which buttons to push. "See? E-5." Annette's chubby little fingers found the buttons under Kenny's watchful eye. The bag of Skittles landed with a rattle and a thud, and she reached in to retrieve them.

"Look, Daddy! I got Skittles!" She shook the red bag in the air and the little candies rustled inside. Ron and Maggie smiled and said something to each other. *They look so happy*, thought Kenny. He wanted them to have some time together.

"Come on, Annette, let's see what else they have…"

"Mostly garbage," the disdainful voice came from behind. Kenny spun around. It was the girl who was sitting behind the Evans family.

"Huh?" Kenny asked, dumbfounded at the girl's intrusion.

"These sandwiches are crap!" she indicated, pointing at the rows of egg salad, ham and cheese, and cold hamburgers that could be heated up in a microwave. "Believe me. I've tried them all." The girl removed her barrettes, smoothed her hair back, and refastened them, all the while holding Kenny's gaze.

Kenny didn't know what to say. He didn't want to be rude, but why was this girl butting in on his business, anyway?

"Are you new here?" she asked. Kenny nodded. "Yeah, I never saw you here before. We usually come up every Sunday." She indicated her mother who was still seated, waiting for the inmate they had come to see. Kenny found his voice.

"How long have you been coming here?"

"A long time. Years. Since second grade. I'm in fifth grade now."

"Me too. In fifth grade, I mean." The girl nodded. Just then Annette interrupted their conversation.

"Kenny! I still want to buy something in this one!" she had her hands pressed against the door, peering in at the treats that would be hers if her brother would just slide a dollar bill or two into the slot and tell her which buttons to push.

"Okay, what do you want?" Kenny asked, unfolding a dollar bill.

"Rice Krispy Treats!" Annette had her face pressed against the glass door now. "Right there. It says F-1. I know how to do it now. I just can't reach where the money goes."

"Okay, here…" Kenny smoothed and inserted the dollar and stepped back so Annette could push the buttons. Annette was enjoying herself immensely.

"My name's Lydia. What's your name?" The new girl was not shy.

"Kenny. My sister's name is Annette." Annette, already eyeing her next purchase, ignored the exchange between Kenny and Lydia. Lydia got her attention.

"Hey, Annette! Stay away from the sandwiches," Lydia warned. "The lunchmeat is made out of recycled garbage, and the mayonnaise is really just some gooey stuff that tastes like glue." Mrs. Juarez's sandwich poem popped into Kenny's mind, and he wondered if Mrs. Juarez had ever eaten sandwiches from a prison vending machine. Annette's eyes opened wide and she stared in disbelief.

"Really?" she whispered.

"Oh, yeah. They scrape all the leftover food from the kitchen and make it into ham and bologna and stuff, and then they sell it in the machines here,"

Lydia replied, her voice confident. "I won't touch 'em, myself. Not anymore. Not since I found out. But plenty of people do. Just stick with chips and candy," Lydia cautioned in a hushed voice. She looked at Kenny and grinned. She sounded so authoritative that he almost believed her, but then he realized she was just messing around with Annette. Kenny didn't know whether to be mad because she was playing a joke on his little sister or to go along with the joke. Suddenly he felt like he needed to laugh.

"Well," Kenny interjected in a serious tone that indicated he believed Lydia and was about to expand on the subject, "my teacher's favorite food is a sandwich even worse than the ones here. I wonder if I should buy one of these and take it back for her." Lydia shook her head.

"I wouldn't. Not unless you want to kill her. Is she a mean teacher?" Annette was spellbound, absorbing the banter as though it were serious dialogue. "I mean, if she's mean, then, sure – take a *couple* back. The 'chicken salad' is the worst," Lydia said, making little quotation marks with her fingers when she said "chicken salad." "It even has *toilet paper* in it!" Annette was clearly horrified.

"Kenny! I don't want any sandwiches," Annette whined softly. Then she turned and sped away, calling out to her parents that she didn't want any sandwiches. Kenny and Lydia broke into a laugh.

"Really, the sandwiches aren't all that bad. I like the hot ones, best, though. You can heat them up in the microwave. They have a rib sandwich sometimes." Lydia seemed to be an authority on the topic of prison visiting room vending machines. Kenny wondered what else he would learn about this girl. Just then the clanging keys alerted them that another prisoner was being escorted into the room.

"Dad!" Lydia bolted away from Kenny and rocketed toward the older man who was just brought in. Lydia's mom followed behind. Kenny couldn't keep from staring. The reunion was such a personal event, but he couldn't help himself, as he felt drawn into the scene. These very private and personal moments were going on all around him in full public view. It seemed wrong somehow.

Kenny could hear Lydia jabbering away to her dad as she showed him all the food she had scored from the machines. "I got your favorites!" she chimed, waving the little bags at him. He looked kind of old to be her dad, Kenny thought. Then Kenny turned back and looked at his own family. Annette sat in between Ron and Maggie talking a mile a minute. His parents looked remarkably happy considering the circumstances. Kenny glanced over and saw Mrs. Curtis, the kind lady who helped them checking in that morning. She was listening intently to her son whose expression was serious as he leaned in close and spoke quickly, in a hushed tone. Kenny couldn't tell what was being said.

Across the way he saw the noisy girl group and the inmates they were visiting. The little baby became cranky as the mother bounced it in her arms, leaning close to her husband or boyfriend or whoever he was. The sassy redhead talked loudly and expressively. She seemed almost to be performing. Suddenly Kenny felt invisible. He continued to look at the people in the room. A guard at the desk spoke into a phone looking bored. Some new people waited outside the visiting room to be admitted. Through the glass door Kenny saw them hold up their stamped hands.

Who are all these people, and why are we all here in prison? Kenny wondered. He looked back at his dad who now held Annette on his lap while engaged in conversation with Maggie. *My dad is in prison*, Kenny thought. *My dad is a prisoner. But he is not a criminal.* Suddenly Kenny felt very tense and angry and confused. He wanted to run. Or wake up and find it was just a dream. He wanted to be anywhere but inside a prison visiting room with his family.

Chapter 13 – How It Happened

"Hey, what are you doing?" Lydia broke in on Kenny's thoughts. He let out a deep sigh.

"Nothing," Kenny stammered, his head down and eyes averted. Lydia eyed his thin frame and reflected for a few seconds. She seemed to be making up her mind about something.

"Listen," Lydia confided, "the first visit sucks. I was lucky I was so little when my dad came to jail, but I remember being scared to death. I thought they were going to keep me, too. And every little thing I did wrong, I was afraid I'd get caught and locked up." Kenny just listened. "I mean, I know you're not thinking stuff like that, but I know you're thinking about stuff… prison stuff." Lydia's confident voice trailed off. Kenny just stood there, a profound sense of gratitude swelled up inside him. Lydia understood. She knew what he was feeling.

"It's just that," Kenny caught himself. He didn't know why her dad was in prison, after all. "It's just that, he didn't do anything wrong. He didn't commit a crime." Lydia looked skeptical, but she was polite.

"Sure, that happens a lot," she offered.

"Well, it happened to us," Kenny went on. He slumped into a vacant chair and Lydia sat down next to him. "This creep named *Len Herd...*" Kenny seethed as he spoke the hated name. "My dad and his friend, Hector, had to switch jobs," Kenny continued, explaining the problems at the fernery. "And somehow they ended up working for this fat, slimy *creep!*" Lydia sensed that Kenny rarely talked about people this way. His hatred for this Len Herd character, though, was certainly unmistakable.

"Well, what did Len Herd do to get your dad put in prison?" Lydia asked matter-of-factly.

"Drugs. Marijuana. Everyone in town knows he's a pothead. But Herd blamed Hector and my dad, and now they're both in prison."

"Well, how?"

"Okay, well, my mom's explained it to me, and I'm not sure how the law works – they're trying to appeal it – that means he can get out and not have a record – but this is what happened..." Kenny took a deep breath and began.

"Every morning Creep Face Len Herd would pick up Hector, and then they would pick up my dad. Like I told you when I explained about them quitting the fernery, Len Herd is a contractor, so my dad and Hector were helping on a new construction project – a strip mall for a dentist and a video store, I think. Anyway, have you ever noticed at construction sites that there is always a box on a post out along the road? It's for the permits, and stuff." Lydia nodded. Several new houses were recently built in Lydia's neighborhood, and she had noticed the boxes.

"Well, contractors also use them to put things in, like keys or the plans... things like that. This one day, Len Herd stopped at another construction site. He said he was checking something for somebody – doing a favor for a friend who had to go out of town – to Las Vegas, I think. Believe me, the only way this creep would do a 'favor' is if there were something in it for him. We figured out later that it was just a lie, that he was just using this other contractor's permit box."

Kenny took another deep breath and looked around. He couldn't believe he was telling all of this to Lydia, someone he had just met. Kenny had never even told it to Gabe or anyone else. But he was on a roll, and it felt good to be telling the story to a sympathetic ear.

"They stopped, and my dad was in the back seat. He always sat in the back because Hector got picked up first. Len Herd was yacking away on his cell phone, and he asked my dad to get out and get whatever it was inside this box – a small package. My dad didn't really pay any attention. Neither did Hector. I guess Len Herd had done it before, so they didn't think anything of it. Well, when my dad got back in the car he asked Hector to put it in the glove box, so my dad handed it to Hector, and Hector put it in the glove box. This all happened in the morning on their way to the job site." Lydia pictured the events as Kenny continued his story.

"My dad didn't think anything about it. In fact, he kind of forgot about it until later. Hector, too. But anyway, at lunchtime they were all three riding together again. Usually my dad and Hector stayed at the site and ate because they always packed their lunch, but Len Herd asked them to go with him. So, they were going down the road when a cop pulled them over. Len Herd was cursing and swearing until the cop came up to him, then he was nice and saying, 'Oh, my stepson is a police officer in Dallas, Texas' and trying to schmooze up the cop. My dad said the cop didn't seem impressed, and he asked Len Herd to get out."

Kenny looked over his shoulder now to make sure no one was listening in. "So how did your dad and Hector get popped?" Lydia was hanging on every word.

"This is the part where we don't know for sure what happened. Maybe Len Herd knew the car was going to be searched. I mean, it was his car, right? But he was outside talking to the cop and my dad said before you knew it two other cop cars rolled in, and next thing they knew, my dad and Hector were being ordered out of the car, too. The cops found marijuana in the package in the glove box, and you *know* that's what Len Herd had to be picking up that morning, but it's my dad and Hector who ended up being accused and convicted! Len Herd said it was *their* package, not his!"

Kenny spoke quickly, the frustration and agony evident in his voice. His dark brown eyes were flashing, and Lydia noticed for the first time the deep, dark circles under his eyes. Lydia glanced back over at Kenny's dad and made a mental note that Kenny looked just like his dad, and Annette looked just like his mom. "Well, how? I mean, didn't they have a lawyer?"

"Kind of. Hector didn't have money to hire a lawyer, and I think my grandparents loaned my parents money to get a lawyer, but my parents said he didn't know what he was doing and really didn't care. And because Dad's fingerprints and Hector's fingerprints were on the package, it made them look guilty. But my dad didn't do anything wrong. He doesn't do drugs, and everyone in town knows Len Herd is just *trash*." Again, Kenny's voice was heated.

"So, what about Hector? How long is he in for? Can they really get an appeal?" Lydia was curious, and she seemed to easily understand the legal concepts Kenny was recently learning.

"Hector's in another prison. I think he got the same sentence as my dad – three years."

"What about Len Herd? Is he in prison, too?"

Kenny thrust his shoulders back and in a strained, tight voice replied, "*Nothing* happened to him. He's running around *free*." Kenny spoke the last word as though he couldn't believe it. Lydia was quiet for a moment, not believing it either.

"Wow!" she sympathized. "Don't you just want to *do* something to him?" Kenny Evans had always been a kind and gentle person. In fact, he still was. But the injustice he perceived against his father evoked an entirely new side of him, a side even Kenny knew was not good.

"Yeah," he whispered softly, "I *hate* him."

Lydia nodded in agreement. "I hate him, too," she agreed in solidarity. "I wish there was a way for him and your dad to change places."

"And Hector, too."

"Yeah, Hector, too."

"Kenny, I want some more snacks!" Annette broke in on their conversation. For some reason Kenny felt immeasurably better, almost lighthearted. The talk with Lydia had done him a world of good.

"Okay," he said, smiling at Lydia as he stood to go with Annette. Lydia smiled back.

"But I don't want any *sandwiches*!" Annette stated emphatically, wrinkling her nose at the thought of recycled garbage. Lydia and Kenny both broke into laughter. Their somber mood had officially passed.

Chapter 14 – Say Goodbye, Gracie

The rest of the visit passed so swiftly Kenny couldn't believe it had actually been a whole day. After the talk with Lydia he spent the rest of the visit with his family and Lydia with hers. Every now and then Kenny would escort Annette to the snack machines, but the focus was on visiting Dad. They talked about school and sports and books. They talked about music and Gram and the yard and Mom's job. They talked about everything but their present reality. Once, Kenny realized he had been sitting there talking about everything under the sun and had momentarily forgotten they were in the prison.

Suddenly there was a signal from the guard's desk. In a monotone voice the guard announced, "The-following-visits-have-fifteen-minutes-remaining." He paused for a breath and proceeded to read the names of the first group of inmates as though it were one long word. "Curtis-Evans-Grolnick-Taylor-Kunkel. Fifteen-minutes."

He sounds like Gram, Kenny thought. *Only bored.*

Annette was antsy and ready to go, and Kenny suddenly realized he felt a little overwhelmed by events of the day. He looked at his mom and dad and realized this was hardest on them. "Come on, Annette," he coaxed, "let's get a snack to take with us." Maggie smiled gratefully as Annette bounced toward the nearly empty machines. Kenny couldn't believe how many snacks had been consumed in the visiting room that day. But a lot of people were there. He had been so engrossed in his own visit that he hadn't fully realized how the place had nearly filled up. In fact, it just occurred to him that it was so noisy in there they had all been leaning toward each other, half-shouting to communicate.

"Hey!" It was Lydia. "I just wanted to say 'bye' since you're getting ready to go. We'll get called in the second group."

"Oh. Well, yeah..." Kenny was putting quarters into a machine for Annette. "Uh, do you come every Sunday?"

"Yeah, usually on Sunday. It's my mom's day off."

"Well, I don't know when we're coming back. It depends on when my mom can get off." Annette was trying to decide between the only two choices left in the machine – pretzels or cheese crackers.

"Well, maybe I'll see you here next time," Lydia sounded hopeful. "It's nice to talk to someone my own age, and besides, my parents always have stuff they want to talk about. Sometimes I go in the playroom and play with the little kids." She nodded in the direction of the play area where six or seven small children shared the meager assortment of toys.

"Yeah. I hope so," Kenny replied.

"Hey," Lydia seemed to be thinking out loud, "we should email each other and keep in touch. You know, about visits." She smiled, pleased at her idea. "Can you memorize my email address? It's Lydia Grace, twelve, twenty-two at yahoo dot com."

"Lydia Grace 1222 at yahoo dot com," Kenny repeated. "Sure. Yeah. I'll email you the next time we're coming." Kenny occasionally emailed his friends. "Is Grace your middle name?"

"Uh huh," Lydia nodded. "It's what my dad calls me. 'Gracie.' He always says, 'Say goodnight, Gracie' from some old movie or something. But at school everyone calls me Lydia."

"Oh," Kenny just realized that he had told Lydia a lot earlier, but he had learned very little about her. Maybe they would become friends. He didn't even know what her dad was in prison for. Suddenly Kenny felt uneasy. After all, not everyone was innocent like his dad. Kenny glanced over at Lydia's parents who looked just as normal as all of his friends' parents, with the small exception that Lydia's dad was wearing prison clothes like his own dad. "Thanks for listening this morning. I didn't find out much about you, I guess." He seemed at a loss for words. He didn't want to come right out and ask why her dad was in prison, but she seemed to sense his question.

"It's okay," Lydia assured him. "I hope your dad gets his appeal. And I hope they do something to Pig-face Len Herd." She smiled. For the tough image she had projected when Kenny first noticed her this morning, Lydia was really very nice. Kenny thought that maybe her attitude was just an act.

"Thanks," he said. "And good luck... uh... with your dad, too." Kenny hoped his remark wasn't inappropriate. After all, he didn't even know why her dad was incarcerated.

Lydia looked down at her shoes. "Thanks," was all she managed. Then she brightened. "Email me! Lydia Grace 1222 at yahoo dot com." She turned, looked back, saluted, and walked away. Kenny laughed. She actually saluted!

C hapter 15 – The Drive Home

Later as the trio rode in the van, the only sound was the passing traffic on the highway. Annette was worn out, her curly head leaned forward, chin resting on her chest as she slept. Kenny and Maggie were quiet, each lost in thought. Maggie and Ron had talked about their hopes for some legal assistance. When Maggie told him about the web site Amy found, Ron told her that several of the inmates he met had spoken very highly of the site as a good resource for inmates and their families. Ron and Maggie decided to post a request for legal assistance to see what might happen. Maggie sighed. She knew Ron was innocent. She constantly wavered between angry and sad. *Len Herd should be the one locked up,* Maggie thought to herself. *He is a conniving liar.*

Traffic was light on Interstate 10. Maggie wondered how many of the cars they saw on the road had been to visit someone at a prison today. Until

Ron's arrest she had no idea what the prison situation in Florida was like, but now she was fully aware that the I-10 corridor was home to more than a half a dozen state prisons, and there were many more throughout the state. Granted, there were plenty of people who belonged in prison, but Maggie wondered how many were innocent, or how many were serving longer sentences because they didn't have money for a good lawyer. Maggie sighed. She certainly knew more about prisons now than she had ever hoped to learn.

Kenny looked out the window. It had been great to see his dad, even under these circumstances. And somehow meeting Lydia had made everything about the day more bearable. Kenny knew that he wouldn't tell his friends about her. They would misunderstand. After all, it wasn't like he had a crush on her or something like that. He just felt better meeting someone his own age that was going through the same thing – visiting her dad in prison. Lydia was funny, too. Even with all of her troubles she had a great sense of humor. Kenny smiled to himself remembering her farewell salute and her big act about the sandwiches. Maybe he would tell Mrs. Juarez about Lydia. Kenny thought about school the next day. Everyone would be talking about Gabe's birthday party at the rock climbing gym. Kenny hoped he wouldn't be asked about why he wasn't there. Of course, if that happened, it meant all of his friends had already discussed it. This thought was somehow worse to him. At least they didn't tease him, like Kelsey had done to Annette. Kenny's size and his gentle nature were two factors in his reluctance to fight, but he knew if anyone ever insulted his dad to his face he would be honor-bound to defend him.

Blink-uh, blink-uh, blink-uh… the turn signal interrupted Kenny's thoughts.

"I thought we'd stop for gas and to stretch our legs," Maggie spoke softly. "We've been driving for a while. Too much sitting for me for one day." She smiled at Kenny who was looking especially tired. "Want a snack or anything?"

"No, I'm not that hungry yet," he replied. He had eaten an egg salad sandwich at the prison just before confessing to a greatly relieved Annette that the sandwiches were safe for human consumption.

"Well, we'll let Annette sleep a little while longer, but I thought we'd stop for dinner in an hour or so. We won't get home until pretty late." Maggie pulled into a convenience store. Kenny jumped out. He liked pumping gas. It made him feel grown up. Maggie handed him the key for the locking gas cap and went in to use the restroom. Kenny unscrewed the cap and began filling. His dad had taught him how to do this, and he was proud of himself. Ron had installed the locking gas cap after someone siphoned almost a full tank one night.

"At these prices we can't take chances," Ron had said. So now every time Maggie stopped for gas she had to unlock the cap first. She knew Kenny felt privileged to pump the gas, so she tried to time it for when he was in the van.

Ten minutes later they were back on the road, Maggie sipping a Diet Coke, Kenny looking out the window, both back to their private thoughts, which, not surprisingly, were quite similar.

Kenny began to wonder about the other inmates. He wondered if there were any murderers in the visiting room today. He wondered about the crimes committed by the inmates. A lot of the men didn't look very old at all – they looked like teenagers. Others, like Lydia's dad, seemed much older. He wondered about Lydia's dad. Maybe he was a murderer. But the inmates had all seemed so normal just sitting there visiting their friends and family, like his family. It didn't feel like a prison at all when you just looked around at the people talking, laughing, sharing stories. It looked more like a reunion.

What if his dad really did have to serve three years? Kenny would be in 8th grade when his dad got out. Eighth grade! That seemed so far off! And what about Lydia? She had been visiting her dad in prison for three years already. She hadn't said anything about how long it would be before he got out. Maybe he was in for life! What would that be like?

Kenny pondered this new world, his thin shoulders hunched over, his elbow on his knee and his chin resting on his hand. His mom had to repeat herself to break in on his thoughts.

"Kenny?"

"Huh?"

"I was just asking about that girl you were talking to today. It seemed like she was trying to make friends with you and Annette." Maggie purposely included the words, "and Annette" so that Kenny wouldn't misinterpret her question.

"Lydia," Kenny acknowledged. "Her name is Lydia Grace. She was visiting her dad. She gave me her email address so I can tell her when we're going up again."

"Oh, that's good," Maggie said. She and Ron had been surprised to notice Kenny in deep conversation with Lydia. He tended to be more reserved when he met someone for the first time. Perhaps his instincts told him something positive about Lydia. Kenny seemed to have stopped abruptly. Maybe he had disclosed too much, or made it sound more personal than it was. Maggie changed gears slightly. "We sure were lucky to meet Mrs. Curtis, too, weren't we?"

"Yeah, she knew the whole signing in thing," Kenny agreed.

"It's funny, but until today I kind of thought as prisons as a place for, well, I don't know, just sort of really bad people, you know?" Kenny nodded as Maggie continued. "I mean, I guess I didn't really think about prisons at all until all of 'this' happened. But I met a very nice lady today, Mrs. Curtis, and Lydia seemed nice, too. And all those other people seemed to be just like everyone else, you know?"

"I know," Kenny agreed, "I was thinking the same thing. I mean, I know Dad shouldn't be there, but I was wondering about everyone else."

"Well, I guess we have a lot to learn about life in prison. Aunt Amy sent me a web site that tries to help families adjust and help inmates, too. I'm going to check into it some more." Her voice sounded hopeful. For a brief, shared moment, Kenny and his mother both felt as though everything was going to turn out fine.

"Look, there's a Cracker Barrel at the next exit. Wanna stop?" Cracker Barrel was a special treat. They usually just ate out at McDonald's or some other fast food place. Kenny brightened thinking about his favorite there – chicken and dumplings.

"Yeah! Can we?"

"Yep, we've had a really nice day so far, and this will top it off." She slowed down as she approached the exit and called softly to Annette who was still napping in the backseat. "Annette… Anneeeeeeeeet-tie… wake up, sweetie, we're going to Cracker Barrel!" Annette also loved Cracker Barrel, especially the gift shop. She stirred and blinked her sleepy eyes, looking out the window as the van pulled in to the parking lot. Suddenly she was wide-awake and full of enthusiasm.

"Can I get a toy?"

"We'll see. Let's think about dinner, first," Maggie laughed.

Three-fourths of the Evans family soon found themselves seated and ordering dinner. A few hours later, the trio pulled into their driveway, tired but happy, their thoughts on Monday morning as it was fast approaching.

Chapter 16 – Funday

All of the students in Mrs. Juarez's class looked forward to Mondays. On their very first day of school in her class, as they went over rules, routines, and procedures, Mrs. Juarez had excited them all with her optimistic and cheerful approach to everything. And one of their favorite announcements came as she discussed attendance policies.

"Research shows that Monday is the worst day for student attendance. In other words, students are more likely to be absent on Mondays than any other day. Now this does not necessarily mean students are more likely to be *sick* on Mondays," she joked, "just *absent.*" Several students laughed knowingly.

"So," she continued, holding up the calendar, "in our class, we will simply *cancel* Mondays!" She drew a big red X over the word "Monday" as students stared quizzically. Hands shot up quickly.

"So we don't have to come to school on Mondays?"

"What are our parents gonna say?"

"Are you serious?"

"You're not serious!"

"Really?"

"*Really?*"

"Coooooooooooool!"

Mrs. Juarez had everyone's undivided attention as she waited patiently for their outburst to subside. As they quieted down she continued.

"Yes, you still have to come to school five days a week, but we are officially replacing Monday with *Funday*," she explained, as though everyone knew what she was talking about. "You see," she went on, "I want you to be as excited about coming to school on Mondays as I am, so by canceling Monday and replacing it with Funday, you *will* be. From now on, on Funday – formerly known as Monday – I personally guarantee you that you will wake up extra early because you will be so curious about the fun surprise that awaits you in the wonderful world of fifth grade!"

A stunned classroom sat puzzling for a moment collecting their thoughts. What could possibly be fun about any day at school, and let's face it, Monday is still Monday no matter what you call it. But some of these students had heard about Mrs. Juarez's unorthodox approaches to engaging her students' interest, so they were cautiously optimistic.

"Every Funday will have something about it that is absolutely fun – a surprise – something you would never expect at school," she promised. "You stick with me on Fundays, and not only will we have a great time, but I predict even your grades will improve because you'll be missing less school." That part certainly made sense to everyone, but there was still an element of suspicion about the whole thing. Curiosity won out, though, and on the following Monday, every single student in Mrs. Juarez's class was present. And they were not disappointed.

As they took their seats and began the routine morning work already written on the board, they were first enthralled by the topics. During DOL – Daily Oral Language – they were expected to identify and correct the mistakes in several sentences written on the board – a routine and sometimes boring activity that served as a brief skills review, but mainly as a way to get them focused on their school day. Today, however, the sentences were all about them. Yes, the spelling, punctuation, and capitalization mistakes waited to be corrected, but the names and places in the sentences referred to people and places they knew. They buzzed as they worked, delighting in recognizing their own names or their classmates' names. There was even a sentence about their principal:

on friday mr joseph announced a field trip
to the central florida zoo

The students had to capitalize and punctuate the sentences, which were suddenly much more interesting than the usual sentences they copied and corrected during Daily Oral Language. Was this the Funday surprise? They quickly finished their work, eager to see what else Funday would bring. They were not disappointed. A box of Munchkins appeared on Mrs. Juarez's desk.

"Boys and girls, as you finish your work, please stop by my desk and try a Munchkin from Dunkin' Donuts."

The students eyed the donuts and grinned at each other. They were so lucky! School was in session only one week, and already they had heard horror stories from their fifth grade counterparts in Mrs. Mercer's class next door.

"Old 'Misery' just complains about everything and gives out worksheets!"

"Mrs. Mercer is always yelling at us!"

"I wish I could be in *your* class!"

Mrs. Mercer's students lamented at recess, at lunch, on the bus – anywhere there was an audience. And Mrs. Juarez's class continued to smile and love school, especially Fundays. There were always several little surprises throughout the day. The students didn't even linger at recess, but hurried back to class to see what else was in store for them. It was hard to explain to anyone who wasn't a student in Mrs. Juarez's class, but one thing was certain: if someone was absent on a Monday, everyone knew that person was really sick.

This morning Kenny arrived at school eager to hear about Gabe's birthday party. He was still feeling good about his visit with his dad, and it was Funday, after all. There was a lot of commotion among the boys when he arrived. They talked about climbing, almost falling, catching each other, and too casually used the new terminology they had picked up, each showing off a bit in his own way.

"Yeah, I had to *belay* for Scott, and I almost dropped him!"

"I thought *bouldering* was way cool…"

"I got tangled in my *harness*…"

And so it went, everyone sharing stories about the event and planning another session as soon as possible. Kenny enjoyed their vivid descriptions and knew he would be included on future trips. His own Sunday adventure had been full of its own excitement, and he was a little surprised that he felt no regret about missing out on the climbing adventure.

"Good morning, everyone," Mrs. Juarez smiled. "I'm so glad that everyone is here today!"

They all grinned. It was Funday. No one would miss if they could help it.

"Today we are beginning 'Newspapers in Education,' a fun way to learn about current events and how these events affect all of us." She had placed newspapers on everyone's desk and encouraged them to spend a few minutes to find something that interested them personally. "The newspaper is not just a bunch of headlines about politicians and faraway places," she explained. "There are stories and features and ideas that I promise you'll like. How many of you already read the newspaper each day?" Students looked around the room at each other, but no one raised their hand. "How about your families?" Mrs. Juarez continued. About half of the students raised a hand now. "Well, I promise, by the time you leave fifth grade you'll not only know *how* to read the newspaper, but you will really enjoy it."

Skepticism was met with optimism. By now these students knew that Mrs. Juarez delivered on her promises. After about five minutes of perusing the newspapers, Mrs. Juarez asked for volunteers to share something of interest.

"The comics!"

"The ads for the movies!"

"The sports section!"

"Here's an article about surfing," Adam exclaimed. "And another about the Kennedy Space Center." Adam Gopnik was interested in everything. His enthusiasm was contagious, and other students began to look more closely at the articles.

Kenny saw a small headline that read, 'Prison population at record high.' The article described the fast rate of growth in Florida's prison population. Of course the article interested him in a tragic way, and he didn't want anyone to see him reading it. He turned the pages and looked for something else. 'Twin-engine Cessna crashes in Keys' caught his eye. He looked over at Rachel Mason whose uncle was a pilot. He saw that she was reading the same article. It wasn't about her Uncle Erik, thank goodness, but he saw Rachel raise her hand to talk about it.

Kenny turned a few more pages and found an article about Florida's state parks. That would do.

After everyone had a chance to describe something of personal interest, Mrs. Juarez continued with the newspaper activity.

"We've been learning a lot about geography, so this morning I want to give you a chance to show off your knowledge." This is always how she approached everything. Not, "Let's see if you remember anything," but "Let's show off your knowledge." No wonder her students admired her. "We're going to play Geography Bingo!" she announced.

Bingo! The students loved to play games. Sheets of paper were quickly distributed. On each paper was printed a blank Bingo card. Mrs. Juarez explained how it would work.

"As you find the name of a city or country in the newspaper, raise your hand. I need a volunteer to write the names." Hands waved. "Alice Lee, will you write each name on a slip of paper?" She handed Alice Lee the slips as raised hands began to wave eagerly. "As the names are called out, you have to spell it slowly so that Alice Lee can write it on a slip of paper and all of you will write it somewhere –

anywhere you want – on your blank Bingo card."
Everyone smiled. They got the idea. "Then, when all
of the blanks are filled up, we'll play Bingo!"

Excitement was in the air as students called
out the places they located in the paper.

"Paris! Capital p, a, r, i, s, Paris!" Haley
Bennington called out. Then she used it in a
sentence, just for good measure. "When I turn
sixteen, my mom's taking me to Paris!" She beamed
at Mrs. Juarez who called on the next student.

"Key West. Capital k, e, y, space, capital w, e,
s, t!"

"Detroit. Capital d, e, t, r, o, i, t, Detroit!"

And so they continued, calling out foreign
cities and countries as well as places more familiar.
Kenny recognized one of the names, Starke, as an exit
they had passed on their way to the prison. It seemed
that there were reminders everywhere of his family's
plight. But his attention was focused on Mrs. Juarez's
engrossing activity.

"There! You should have every square filled
in with the name of a place. Now, we'll pull out the
slips one by one, and as soon as you have Bingo,

either horizontally, vertically, or diagonally," she drew lines on the board as a quick review, "you'll call out Bingo!   However, to actually *win* at Bingo, once you've gotten it, you have to come up to the maps and point out the five locations that are in your Bingo."

The class *ooohed* and *aaahed*.   This was an unexpected challenge, and there was a real air of excitement now.   Who was the best geography student?   Who had been the most places?   They all peered at the three maps located at the front of the room – a Florida map, a U.S. map, and a world map. This was going to be fun!

The first name was pulled.   California. Everyone marked it off where they had printed it on a Bingo square. Tallahassee. Paris. Germany. New York. Key West. Canada. Mexico. Starke. On it went, the steady reading of the slips, until the excited whispers began.

"I only need one more!"

"Cuba! Say 'Cuba!'"

"Man, oh, man, I still need three. I'm not getting anything here!"

Suddenly Rachel tentatively called, "Bingo!"

"Awwwwwwwwwwww..." the whole class moaned in unison.

"Good for you, Rachel! Now you have to come up and show us on the maps where all of these places are located."

Uh-oh! Here was the challenging part! A lot of the places were easy, but there were some unfamiliar places as well.

"You'll have three minutes to point to all five locations," Mrs. Juarez instructed, setting the timer on her desk. Rachel walked forward quickly. Everyone watched closely just in case she missed any. At least they might learn some places they didn't already know. Rachel quickly pointed out Canada and Paris on the world map, eventually found Detroit on the U.S. map, but ran out of time before locating Starke and Punta Gorda in the Sunshine State. A bit disappointed, she returned to her seat for the game to continue. Students were flipping through books in their desks trying to locate places they were unsure of.

"Okay, we'll keep playing," Mrs. Juarez continued. There was a renewed interest and new element of apprehension. You couldn't just win by having Bingo. You had to find these places on the maps! Oh, boy!

"Afghanistan…"

A few groans escaped as the tension mounted.

"Savannah…"

"Bingo!" It was Kenny, jubilant and on his feet. Classmates encouraged and joked.

"You'll find them!"

"No fair! Rachel already did most of the work for you!"

"Miss one! Miss one!"

Mrs. Juarez allowed the good-natured remarks. Everyone was thoroughly involved and searching the maps. The timer was ticking, and Kenny began. Canada. Savannah. New York. Paris. All that was left was Starke. Kenny moved to the Florida map and began scanning the northern region. He knew it was here somewhere. His classmates continued their friendly taunts.

"Look in Australia!"

"He doesn't know!"

"Come on, Kenny!"

"It's in Cuba! Look in Cuba!"

He remembered the road signs going both directions yesterday and knew that Starke was located between Jacksonville and Tallahassee. He scanned slowly, sure it was somewhere between the two cities.

"Thirty seconds!"

"He's not going to make it!"

"I can see it from here!"

Suddenly, there it was. Starke! Kenny pointed and called out, "Here it is!" The class cheered and groaned simultaneously. Geography Bingo was a huge success. Mrs. Juarez was grinning at the class.

"Congratulations, Kenny!" she said as he took his seat. "How were you able to narrow it down to such a specific region?" Mrs. Juarez liked to "tap into prior knowledge" as she called it. Kenny felt a few behemoth butterflies boxing in his stomach. *Think fast!*

"Oh, uh, that was a lucky guess. I think maybe I saw it on a map once." He certainly had no intentions of revealing his drive along Interstate 10 the day before.

"Well, whatever strategy you used, you did fine. You too, Rachel. So, did you learn anything this morning?" she quizzed the class. As the students expounded on their new love for the newspaper and geography in general, and Geography Bingo specifically, Kenny retreated to La La Land for a few minutes remembering the long trip yesterday, and more specifically, the reason for it. He would be sure to write his dad a letter and tell him all about Geography Bingo. He also vowed to himself to start reading the newspaper. Not just to learn about geography, but Kenny had discovered a whole new subject of interest – prisons.

C hapter 17 – What's New?

That afternoon Maggie picked up Kenny and Annette in Gram's car. That meant only one thing – the minivan was back in the repair shop for something or other. Kenny kept his opinions to himself when he got in the car, but Annette began complaining right away.

"Mommy! Where's our car? Gram's car stinks like cigarettes!" Maggie couldn't disagree. She had rolled all the windows down hoping to alleviate some of the smell.

"Sorry, kids. I guess that long drive yesterday didn't agree with the van. Don't worry. It should just be a day or two at the most." Kenny felt badly for his mom and wondered how much the repairs would cost. He knew that Gram helped out financially sometimes, and although his dad's parents had even less money, they occasionally sent a small check to help out. They lived in Michigan, so Kenny rarely saw them.

"But, whenever there's bad news, good news is bound to follow," Maggie continued. Something was up! Kenny thought that his mom seemed in happier spirits than she ought to, what with the van needing repairs. It was his dad! His dad was getting out of prison!

"What's the good news?" he asked, amazed that Mom hadn't just blurted it out, or come and checked them out of school early to tell them right away. "Is it about Dad?"

"Well," Maggie's face flickered a moment as she realized what her son was hoping, "it's *kind* of about Dad in a roundabout way. This morning Ryan asked me if I wanted to become the front-end manager. It would mean more money, days only, and I'd only have to work one Sunday a month!"

The magnitude of this announcement was not lost on Kenny. He knew what this meant for their family – more money, which they sorely needed, evenings with Mom at home, and three Sundays a month to visit Dad, guaranteed! Wow! No wonder Mom was not acting disappointed about the repairs.

"That's really cool, Mom! That is *really* good news!" Kenny felt a surge of pride for his mom. A promotion! Ryan, her store manager, was promoting her. This would be a big help to the family in so many ways. "Congratulations! Congratulations on your promotion!"

"Thank you," Maggie beamed at her son who was wise beyond his years. Kenny recognized that it was far more than a job promotion, but would provide real benefits for their family. "I'm so excited. I get trained this week, and next week I'll start. The new schedule will take effect after that, so in three weeks we'll go back to visit Daddy." She always referred to Ron as "Daddy" to the kids.

"Mommy, can Kelsey come along when we visit Daddy? She's sorry now, and I told her I would buy her something in the machine." Annette's first grade world was so simple.

"No, baby, Kelsey can't come, but maybe she can come over after school some day to play. I'll call Kelsey's mommy on the phone and ask."

Kenny felt happy. His mom's promotion was big news, and he'd had such a great day at school. He was eager to tell her about it. First he described the Geography Bingo. By now all of the families in Mrs. Juarez's class understood about Funday, and they looked forward to hearing about the surprises Mrs. Juarez had in store for her students. Maggie listened excitedly and was proud to hear how Kenny had won. She made a mental note to bring a roadmap along on their next visit to see Ron so that Kenny would have the opportunity to practice his map skills. Then Kenny told her the most important part of the day.

"There's a D.A.R.E. essay contest," he told her. "Officer Randall announced it and gave us the guidelines. Mrs. Juarez talked to me later and said that I was one of the best writers she's ever had in her class." Kenny spoke humbly. "She said my *Florida Writes!* score from fourth grade was the highest she'd ever seen, and that she really loved that story I wrote when we did the unit on westward expansion." Kenny smiled remembering the fictional account he wrote of meeting Laura Ingalls Wilder. He wrote from the perspective of a little field mouse that resided with the pioneer family and called his story, "Little Mouse on the Prairie." The entire class had loved it when Kenny read his story from the Author's Chair.

"Anyway," Kenny continued, "I think I have a good idea for the contest, and I've decided to enter." At this pronouncement he took a deep breath and looked at his mom expectantly. *My goodness,* Maggie thought, *was this the same boy who couldn't stand the sight of the D.A.R.E. officer just a couple of weeks ago?*

Annette, who had not been the center of attention for entirely too long now suddenly interrupted with her version of the day's major events. "Emily threw up in my class today, and Mrs. Morton let me take her to the nurse. It's because I'm the nurse helper this week. It's my job to be nice." Kenny and Maggie both suppressed the urge to laugh when Annette said that it was her job to be nice. It just sounded funny the way she said it.

"That's nice, honey. Was Emily okay after she went to the nurse?"

"Probably because her daddy came and took her home. We made a card for her and I drew a red flower on it. Because red is Emily's favorite color. And it's my favorite color, too."

The conversation ended abruptly as Maggie pulled in the driveway in a sudden panic. A police car was parked in their driveway! Something was wrong!

Kenny felt his stomach grow sick, and he was afraid that he would be throwing up in a minute like Emily had done at school. What happened? What was wrong? Maggie was in a daze as she parked Gram's car and got out, unable to speak. She moved slowly, as if in a dream, Kenny behind her. *It must be something to do with Dad*, he thought. *Something else must have gone wrong.*

Maggie was remembering the web site she had visited and imagined the worst: a police officer had been dispatched to tell her that Ron had been severely beaten in prison. *Oh, my god*, she thought, *where is the officer?* She sent up a silent prayer – *Please let Ron be okay.* As Maggie walked toward the house she still saw no sign of the police officer other than the patrol car parked in the driveway. The nightmare of Ron's arrest was flooding back over all of them. Even Annette seemed afraid, gripping her mother's hand tightly and not saying a word. Kenny brought up the rear, his legs like lead, his head spinning with fear and confusion.

Suddenly the back door opened, and Gram came out on the small deck, a police officer chatting pleasantly with her. Gram blew a puff of cigarette smoke and laughed at whatever the officer had said. *"Don't-you-worry,"* she assured the officer, *"you-better-believe-we-will!"* Maggie, Kenny, and Annette stopped in their tracks as the officer made his way towards them and on to his car.

"Hah ya'll dune?" he drawled. They nodded dumbly as the officer looked back at Gram and cautioned, "Aw-rat, Ah'm gonna check with y'all in a few days and make sure y'all got that thang fixed. Take-keh, now!" He waved as he climbed into his cruiser and backed out of the driveway. Maggie let out her breath. So did Kenny and even Annette who tended to be less attuned to such distractions.

"What's going on?" Maggie asked Gram.

"Awwww," Gram began, waving her lit cigarette in the direction of the door, *"I-forgot-about-that-stupid-lock-not-working-half-the-time, and-I-locked-myself-*

out-for — what? — the-umpteenth-time. I-was-trying-to-climb-in-the-living-room-window," Gram inhaled deeply on her cigarette before continuing, *"when-that-cop-drove-by-and-thought-I-was-breaking-in!"* Gram blew out a puff of smoke. No one interrupted as she finished with a flourish. *"I-explained-everything, and-then-he-got-the-door-open-for-me. You-gotta-get-that-fixed!"* she exclaimed. And then, as though nothing at all had happened, Gram looked at Kenny and Annette and asked sweetly, *"And-how-was-your-day?"*

Chapter 18 – The Contest

"Mom, can I use the computer to do so some research for my essay?" Kenny had been working on the essay for over a week now, and he had thought of a few questions he should try to find the answers for.

"Sure, honey," Maggie answered. "What kind of research are you trying to do?"

"Well, I want to find out some prison statistics," he answered a little sheepishly. Kenny knew his mom would support him in any topic he chose to write about, and now that he was really on a roll he wanted to make sure he covered all the bases.

"That's a good idea," she nodded thoughtfully. "You know... I think..." her voice trailed off as she went over to the computer and looked over Kenny's shoulder as he logged on to the Internet. "Can I show you something?" Maggie asked. "I think it might help."

"Sure," Kenny was grateful for her interest, "I was just going to start with Google."

"Well, remember I told you about that web site Aunt Amy sent? They have a lot of prison statistics there." Maggie typed in 'writeaprisoner.com' and then said, "Yep. This is it." Kenny saw the warning that the site was for adults only. He was a long way from turning eighteen. He looked quizzically at his mom when she clicked on 'enter.' "It's okay," Maggie assured her son. I'm logging on, and you're not contacting inmates. I'm just trying to help you find the information you want."

She clicked on a link, and instantly a page full of statistics popped up. Together she and Kenny read through them, trying to determine which were most useful for what he was writing. Kenny and Maggie were both stunned to read these frightening statistics about prisoners. But Maggie believed that this writing project was important for Kenny, and she was determined to help to this small degree. Once he had the information they logged off the site, and Kenny suddenly thought about Lydia. He had never emailed her like he promised! Everything had been kind of hectic since the visit, and now he knew the next time they were going to see Dad. He typed in her email address and wondered if he had remembered it correctly. Maybe he should just send a test email to be on the safe side.

Hi Lydia – is this the right address? This is Kenny from – here he hesitated – *the visiting room. Have you had any chicken salad lately?*

There! That was a safe test message. He hit 'send' and wondered if he would hear back from her any time soon.

Kenny went back to his room and continued working on the essay. He was deep in thought and hard at work when his mom knocked on his door an hour or so later.

"How's it going? Homework all done?"

"Awww, my homework!" he crowed. "I forgot all about it. I was writing my essay."

Maggie saw the pages spread across the bed. There were lots of crossed out sections as Kenny wrote and rewrote. He always enjoyed the editing process and finding just the right words to convey his meaning.

"I guess I'll work on this some more tomorrow," Kenny sighed, reluctantly gathering up his papers. "At least all I have for homework is math, and we have to come up with an idea for a newspaper editorial." Mrs. Juarez had been expanding the Newspapers in Education activities, and lately they had been reading letters to the editor so they could learn how to write their own. Kenny already had a few ideas for that.

"Okay, well, I won't disturb you since you have work to do. I'm glad I interrupted you when I did, though," Maggie smiled, pulling the door shut behind her as she went out.

Thirty minutes later Kenny's homework was finished and stowed safely in his backpack. He went out to the kitchen to see if dinner was ready. His mom was just taking something out of the oven. Her mood was light. The promotion at work had really had a positive impact for her. Maggie was also excited because she and Leticia had sent off a request for legal assistance to the web site Amy had steered her towards. The two wives frequently kept in touch since both of their husbands shared the same fate. Maggie remained hopeful. She had to.

"Just in time!" she called out to Kenny as he slid across the floor in his socks, something he had enjoyed doing practically since he learned to walk. He screeched to a halt at the snack bar where he and Annette liked to eat. "Is pizza okay with you?" Maggie and Kenny both grinned. Pizza was one of his favorite foods, especially what they fondly referred to as "box pizza." All of the ingredients came in a box, and Maggie mixed the crust and made the pizza herself.

"It'll have to do, I guess," Kenny jokingly complained. "If only you'd make Brussels sprouts more often." Kenny sighed, pretending to be disappointed with the pizza his mom had made. The phone rang, and Kenny slid across the kitchen floor to answer it.

"Hello?" Kenny listened for a moment, then covered the receiver with his hand. "Mom," he called softly, "it's Dad." Kenny pressed "1" to accept the collect call.

"Dad! Hi, Dad! How are you?" Kenny was smiling tentatively.

"Oh, I'm fine, son. How are you? How's school?"

The two chatted while Maggie put dinner on the table. Kenny described the essay he was writing. He had become much more comfortable talking to his dad about the "situation," as they called it.

"I'm really proud of you, Kenny. It sounds like a great essay, and I can't wait to read it." Maggie was signaling the time, pointing to her watch. The calls from the prison had to be short, so Kenny said goodbye and handed the phone over to his mom. He heard her excitedly describing the legal request she and Leticia had posted on the Internet as he went to call Annette to the phone. Maggie always let both kids have a turn on the phone, so she tended to talk quickly in order to share the time.

Later that evening as Kenny finished up his essay, he thought about Lydia and wondered if she had written back. His mom and Annette were busy cutting out pictures for a scrapbook Annette wanted to make, so no one was using the computer. He logged on to check his email, and sure enough, there was a message from Lydia.

Hey – thanx for writing – I thought you might forget my addy. Whats new – are you coming to visit this sunday? Is Anette (sp???) still afraid of chicken salad? LOL!!!

It was just a short message, but Kenny was happy to read it. Somehow there was comfort in having a friend – was Lydia a friend? – who was going through the same kind of thing he was. Kenny hit "reply" and answered right away.

Not this Sunday. My mom got a promotion at work. She works at Publix. So, in two weeks we're coming up. And then she'll only have to work one Sunday a month.

Kenny hesitated. Should he write more? Lydia had asked him what was new. He felt a connection to Lydia and wanted to exchange email in between visits, but he wasn't sure how to proceed. Kenny's fingers tapped out a few words, deleted them, tapped a few more, and then sat motionless as he contemplated what to do. He was curious about Lydia, about prison life, about Lydia's dad, about lots of things, but he was also too polite to just ask. Okay, so he would just go with "what's new."

My grandmother locked herself out of the house the other day and the cops caught her climbing in the window.

No. He deleted the words. He really didn't want to write about the police.

We're having a D.A.R.E. essay contest at school. Do you have D.A.R.E. at your school?

He was still on the subject of police, so he deleted again. Oh well. He continued.

I forgot to tell my teacher about the great sandwiches. Annette has been asking about the ingredients in everything she eats. At dinner tonight she was suspicious of the cheese on the pizza. LOL! That's the news here. Not much. How about you? What's up?

Kenny read it over and decided it didn't sound too stupid. He hit the "send" button and felt okay about it. Kenny looked forward to hearing back from Lydia. He was sure she would respond. He thought about it for a few minutes – how much they seemed to have in common — and decided Lydia would be a pretty good friend to have.

C hapter 19 – "And the winner is…"

The classroom buzzed with excitement. Today Officer Randall was going to announce the winner of the essay contest. Kenny had felt all along like he had a pretty good chance, but he also knew there were some other good writers in his class – Rachel Mason and Adam Gopnik, for instance.

Kenny felt very fortunate to be in this class. Most of his classmates were a lot like him – they enjoyed the challenges Mrs. Juarez planned for them, and there was the occasional air of competition, like with this essay contest. Of course, D.A.R.E. was not something Mrs. Juarez planned, but her writing projects and writing centers helped everyone hone their skills.

Kenny's favorite writing center was the one for Creative Writing. There were always several good ideas for writing projects, and Mrs. Juarez encouraged students to submit their writing for publications.

Kenny's work had been published several times, and although he appeared remarkably humble about this achievement, he was secretly very pleased and proud. Rachel Mason was a great writer, but she never submitted anything for publication despite Mrs. Juarez's coaxing. Adam was new to their class having moved to the area just recently. His skills as a writer were evident. He had already submitted a story to *Stone Soup* and was waiting to hear if it was accepted for publication.

"You know you're gonna win!" Haley was reassuring Rachel who wore a nervous smile. She looked hopeful, but shook her head.

"No, probably not. Mine wasn't that good." In her heart Rachel knew she had not made much of an attempt. The subject wasn't one she really wanted to write about. And hadn't Mrs. Juarez, after all, always encouraged them to pursue their interests? No, Rachel was not expecting to win. "*You* might win," she suggested to Haley, although not very convincingly.

"Ha! Fat chance! If you don't win, it's gotta be Kenny or Adam." Haley was realistic. She knew her writing was only so-so.

Kenny looked down at the book on his desk. He didn't want to be caught eavesdropping. Still, he was pleased that his name was mentioned.

Rachel and Haley got back to work. They, like Kenny, were on "Yo-Yo" time. Yo-Yo time was Mrs. Juarez's solution for what students could do when they finished an assignment early. Yo-Yo stood for, "You're on your own." She had a poster on her wall with a picture of a yo-yo, along with several suggestions for ways to keep students busy instead of bored. A few of the suggestions were permanent and never came off the list:

> Read anything you want
>
> Clean out that messy desk
>
> Visit an open center

The other suggestions were modified depending on current topics:

> Rehearse readers' theatre
>
> Illustrate your science adventure story
>
> Make a "Thinking of You" card for Maddie

Find a song to go with your story

Write a "letter to the editor"

Write a "thank you" letter to someone who deserves it

Kenny had finished his assignment and was trying to read *Flush*. He had enjoyed Carl Hiaasen's other book, *Hoot*, and couldn't understand why he was having a hard time focusing now. He was more excited about the essay contest than he wanted to admit. Suddenly, the door opened, and the chatter grew even more heightened,

"Oh, here he is!"

"Hey, Officer Randall! How 'dare' you interrupt our studying?"

"Rachel won, right? Come on, just tell us, did Rachel win?"

Mrs. Juarez shushed them with a smile and her "look" – the one that conveyed much:

I know you're excited, and I understand, but we need to show our respect to our guest. To the D.A.R.E. officer she said, "Welcome to our very excited classroom, Officer Randall! As you can tell, we are *very* eager to hear from you today!"

Pat Randall grinned broadly as he strode to the front of the class. He evidently enjoyed his job. "Well, this class was the toughest class of all. Out of all of the fifth grades I visit, there were more excellent essays from this class than any other. It sure made my job hard."

Kenny's heart sank a bit when he heard this. The competition was fiercer than he originally thought. The class was giddy, though, lapping up the compliment. Mrs. Juarez couldn't help showing her pride, either.

"Okay," Officer Randall began as he placed his briefcase on Mrs. Juarez's desk, "I know the suspense is just killing you all!" He prolonged the agony a bit, popping first one lock open, then the other.

"Come on, come on!" several students called out.

"Aw, man, you're killing us, alright! Who won?"

Officer Randall slowly removed their essays from his briefcase. His large hand gripped them in one fat pile, and he held it up over his head.

"Ladies and gentlemen, if these essays are any indication, then I have satisfactorily done my job. You have made some impressive statements. You have made some life changing promises. You have taken a stance against something that never gives, but only takes. And, you have made me very proud."

Even the most restless student sat very still now. Officer Randall's praise was sincere, they could tell. Sometimes adults tried to impress them with a lot of empty talk, but Mrs. Juarez's students could tell the difference. This was authentic praise from someone who had warned them, cautioned them, shown them the dangers of substance abuse. And now Officer Randall was clearly impressed by their offerings to him.

"I'm going to work a bit backwards," he said. "I have three awards – first, second, and third place. And I'd like to begin by introducing our third place winner..." He paused for dramatic effect. The entire class froze.

"Adam Gop..., uh, Gopnik." Cheers went up around the room. Adam, although he was relatively new to the class, had become popular instantly with his kind ways and engaging personality. He was very adult-like for a fifth grader. No one begrudged him – the new boy – an award. Adam smiled and with shoulders back and head held high walked to the front of the room, surprising the D.A.R.E. officer by extending his hand to shake.

"Congratulations, Adam! Well done!"

"Way to go, Adam!" Mark Langdon high-fived him on his way back to his seat, Adam displaying his certificate proudly. "I won't tell anyone you copied off of me," Mark kidded. Adam swung into his seat and smiled across the aisle at Rachel before looking over at Kenny and making a thumbs-up sign. Kenny smiled hesitantly. He was hopeful and nervous at the same time.

"Okay, next, I'm proud to announce the second prize winner..." Officer Randall looked around the room building suspense before announcing, "...Danny Fitzgerald!"

"What the..."

"Whoa! Danny!"

"No way! *Danny?*"

The whole class – Danny included – was stunned. Danny Fitzgerald was certainly capable of writing a winning essay, but he had a reputation for taking the easy way out on assignments, so he was the last person anyone would expect to put his heart into an extra credit kind of assignment like this. Kenny's heart sank. He looked over at Rachel, but she, like her dumbfounded classmates, was busy staring at Danny who was now walking up to the front of the classroom.

I'll never win, now, Kenny thought. *That would make it three boys winning, and it's just not going to happen.* Danny Fitzgerald. Go figure. Danny, normally boastful, smiled shyly and received his award.

"Congratulations, Danny," Mrs. Juarez smiled warmly, careful not to show the abject surprise she was feeling.

"Thanks, Miss Juarez." Danny always called her "Miss" instead of "Mrs." It was just one of the many ways that he appeared careless to his classmates. Now they were looking at Danny differently, each wondering what else they had misjudged him on.

Officer Randall drew himself up to his full uniformed height and surveyed the spellbound students. "Ladies and gentlemen, sometimes, just when I think I've done my job, someone comes along and gently – or *not* so gently – gets my attention. The first place winner in your class has done just that. I believe I've taught you a lot about the dangers of substance abuse. Your essays, at least, indicate that I have done so. However, one of you has taken the message in an important direction, and I am going to ask if the first place winner will read the winning essay aloud."

Rachel and Kenny both squirmed miserably. Why didn't he just say the name and get it over with? Kenny knew it would be Rachel. Three boys? No way.

"Kenny Evans." Officer Randall looked directly at Kenny. "Would you be so kind as to read your winning essay to the class?"

Kenny was stunned. All around him he heard congratulatory remarks, but he was in a daze. He was even too stunned to look at Rachel. If he had, he would have seen Rachel smiling a genuine smile of congratulations. There were no hard feelings on her part.

"Author's Chair!" someone called out.

"Yeah, Kenny, you have to read from the Author's Chair!"

Mrs. Juarez had a wonderful chair that was indeed painted with the words, "Author's Chair" across the back, and it was only used when someone read his or her original work to the class. No one ever sat in it for any other reason. It was a deeply respected class policy. Kenny had sat in it often, wowing his classmates with scary stories of haunted video games, tales of a rugged pioneer mouse, and a fantastic story about a pair of dentures with super-hero characteristics. His stories were always imaginative. Far out. Creative. But this was an entirely new kind of writing.

The class waited. Would there be a super-hero who battled drug dealers? Would there be a super-villain putting drugs in school lunches? What was the "important direction" Officer Randall was talking about?

Kenny perched his lean frame on the seat of the Author's Chair. It sat higher than the other chairs, and Kenny could see out over his classmates if he were so inclined. But he couldn't look at them right now. His dark head was bent over his paper, his shoulders hunched and tense. He read softly, but everyone heard:

You're Known by the Company You Keep

More people are in prison than ever before in American history. And most of the men and women in prison are there because of drug and alcohol related situations. In fact, going to prison has become so common that the government predicts one of every ten men will be locked up at least once in his lifetime. That means that in our class, at least one of the boys is almost certain to go to jail someday.

Kenny paused for a breath while this bit of somber information made its impact. There was no joking around about who it might be. No kidding or name-calling or pointing. Instead, every student looked around the room quickly and mentally counted the number of boys in the class. Thirteen. Kenny continued:

In Florida alone there are about one hundred thousand people in state prisons. In the entire country there are more than two and a half million people locked up. And the majority ended up in prison because of something to do with substance abuse. The statistics are frightening, not just because they are such big numbers, but because each number represents a person, and each person is connected somehow to other people. That means that millions of friends and families are also being "punished" for these drug related situations.

Kenny was deep into his subject now. He kept his head lowered as he read steadily, his voice rising slightly as though the magnitude of what he, too, was hearing was simply unbelievable. The boys and girls, even Officer Randall and Mrs. Juarez listened intently.

Our class has been very fortunate to learn about the effects of substance abuse. Even our teacher teaches us to take care of our health with good nutrition and exercise. Because we are intelligent people – Kenny looked up for the first time at his peers, his thin face serious and intent – *I believe that not one of us will ever experiment with addictive substances like tobacco, alcohol, and drugs. We all know there is nothing to gain from abusing our bodies in this way. But what about other people?   What about people we know, people we meet? What about people we go to school with, or people we work with someday?*

We can't be responsible for other people.   We can only be responsible for ourselves.   Sure, no one in our class will ever do these things, but what about the people we hang out with? Aren't we known by the company we keep?   Even at school other kids say, 'Oh, there goes Mrs. Juarez's class,' in a way that puts a label on us.   We've even talked about how it feels to have a label, even one as positive as being the 'smart kids.' Well, what about all of the other people we end up spending time with?   If we are seen on a soccer field, people will judge us to be soccer players, even if we are out there looking for four-leaf clovers.   If we are seen backstage, people might jump to the conclusion that we are actors, even if we are just there to help move the scenery, and if we are seen with people who abuse drugs and alcohol, people will think we are substance abusers, too.

Chance and probability lessen the risk of this happening, and the surest and best way to reduce the chances of ending up as a prison statistic is to never do anything illegal in the first place.   We already know that. But, there is a phrase — guilty by association — and it's one everyone should think about.

It has to do with the company we keep. We really <u>are</u> known by the company we keep. In addition to living within the law, we should be careful how we choose our friends, and be careful not to put ourselves in risky situations.

Kenny took one last deep breath, squared his hunched shoulders, and looked quickly around the room before finishing.

It's not enough to take a pledge to remain drug free, to promise never to abuse substances, to live within the law. We have to choose our companions carefully so that we don't end up in the wrong place at the wrong time, a victim of circumstance. Because there is no guarantee that we will get a second chance.

Kenny stood and faced Officer Randall, smiling bravely as he accepted his award. He felt good. Physically, he felt exhilarated, as though he had just taken a much needed deep breath after being underwater for too long. Applause rang in his ears as he took his seat, clutching the award. Kenny was happy, relieved, and much too distracted listening to his classmates' congratulations to notice the tears streaming down Mrs. Juarez's smiling face.

C hapter 20 – Hopes and Plans

Finally, they were almost to the prison. That first awkward visit seemed to have taken place so long ago. This morning neither Kenny nor Maggie felt the level of apprehension that they had experienced during their first trip.

"Here we are," Maggie announced, pulling into the prison parking area. Kenny looked around for Mrs. Curtis's car but didn't see it. He had no idea what kind of car Lydia's mom drove. Maggie, Kenny, and Annette made their way to the registration room. *At least we know the drill,* Kenny thought.

They were the only visitors in the room. The same two guards were on duty – the older, matter-of-fact guard, and the younger, friendlier guard. Maggie couldn't help feeling tense even though she was familiar with the routine. She had the family's spending money clutched in a clear Ziploc bag, her driver's license, and her ignition key.   Kenny and Annette carried nothing.

"Do we get a teddy bear stamp, Mommy?" Annette, too, remembered the routine.

"We'll see," Maggie smiled nervously at the older guard, holding her hand out for the stamp. After he stamped Maggie's hand with the ultraviolet ink he held the bottom of the stamp up to Annette so she could see it.

"I wanted a teddy bear," Annette pouted, "not a smiley face."   Annette pressed her face into Maggie's leg.

"Aw, come on... It's always a different stamp so you'll have a surprise."   The older guard spoke with a new tone of gentleness that surprised Kenny. Annette quietly extended her chubby little hand for the stamp.   Maggie and Kenny breathed a sigh of relief.

Within a few minutes the three entered the visiting room.   Kenny scanned the room for Lydia, but she was not there yet.   They had exchanged occasional emails, so he knew the plan was to visit today.   Kenny recognized just one person from their first visit. Still, it was early, and Kenny sensed it would soon become the noisy reunion he had experienced a few weeks ago. A different guard than the one they encountered on their first visit indicated where they should sit to wait for Dad. It was a different spot than last time. These small changes – the stamp, the seating, the different guard – increased Kenny's nervousness a bit. There was comfort in familiarity, and anything new about this situation, however accidental, slightly unnerved him.

"I want a snack," Annette announced. Kenny sighed. Yes, some things changed, but other things always stayed the same. He smiled at his mom who nodded and handed Kenny the plastic bag full of spending money.

"Remember, Lydia told us to buy the good stuff first before the other people get it, so we should buy all of the Skittles first," Annette cautioned. Maggie smiled.

"Honey, you can't just eat Skittles. Buy a snack for yourself and one for Daddy, and then later on you and Kenny can buy some more stuff." Annette skipped to the vending machines and stood entranced at the bountiful selection. Her impulse was to buy Skittles, but her curiosity about the other packaged delights held her attention for a full five minutes before she finally settled on a package of little chocolate donuts. As she pressed the buttons, Kenny looked up to the sound of jangling keys.

"Dad!" Ron nodded and smiled as the guard escorted him to the desk where he was checked in. Maggie, Kenny, and Annette rushed forward to wait impatiently, and in a few seconds the four were locked in a tangled embrace.

"Wanna donut, Daddy?" Annette waved a chocolate donut as the family made their way back to their seating area. Ron was grinning broadly, clearly delighted to be reunited with his wife and children.

"Kenny, I'm so proud about your essay! And everything else! I've been bragging to everyone about you!" Kenny smiled proudly. A lot had happened since he won the D.A.R.E. essay contest.

"So am I," Maggie smiled, leaning against Ron and holding his hand. "We're both so proud of you. It seems like we keep having more and more good news all the time."

"Yeah, like your promotion, Mom. That was pretty big news, too!" Kenny directed the limelight towards his mother, who really was keeping everything all together during this greatest crisis they had ever faced as a family. Kenny truly admired his mom.

"What about me, too?" Annette inquired, never doubting the response.

"Of course we're proud of you, sweetie pie! You are the most *bee-yoo-tee-full* daughter in the whole wide world! You make us proud every day with everything you do!" Maggie turned to Ron. "You should have seen what a good job she did taking care of Melvin!"

Melvin was the first grade mouse. Actually, he was a stuffed mouse, and one of the weekly jobs Mrs. Morton assigned – and the most sought after – was taking care of Melvin. So, for one week, from Monday to Monday, Annette brought Melvin home and took care of him. Parents were asked to write in Melvin's diary the events of each evening, so every night mother and daughter would write, "Dear Diary…" and provide the exciting details of watching

Clifford the Big Red Dog on TV or visiting friends or going shopping. Occasionally a parent would include Melvin in some grand adventure, like a trip to Disney World, but most of Melvin's escapades were rather predictable.

During the school day Melvin accompanied his caretaker to every destination. He went to P.E. and art and music, and even Mr. Joseph, the principal would say to the student carrying him, "Hi, Justin… hi, Melvin." The first graders demanded worksheets and assignments for Melvin, and happily did double assignments to help their mousey friend. Melvin even had his picture taken on picture day, and Mrs. Morton ordered 24 wallet-sized photos. On the back of each she inscribed, "With love, from your friend, Melvin" and placed one on the desk of every student.

"When Samantha had Melvin he got dirty, and Mrs. Morton had to wash him," Annette tattled. "He didn't get dirty when I took care of him." Ron and Maggie grinned at each other as Ron gently caressed his daughter's blond curls.

"I'm sure Melvin loved staying with you!" Ron assured her.

"Hey, what's up?" It was Lydia, leaning over the seats and grinning widely at Kenny and Annette. Lydia had arrived!

"Hi, Mr. Evans. Hi, Mrs. Evans. I'm Lydia." She extended her hand, surprising both parents. Lydia was very sure of herself. "Hey, Annette, let's get some chicken salad sandwiches!" Lydia laughed.

Annette scrunched up her nose and then laughed. "You can't trick me again!" she said defensively. She looked slyly at Lydia. "And guess what else?" Annette seemed to be contemplating something serious. "All of the Skittles are hot and will burn your tongue. So don't buy them!" Everyone howled at this outburst.

"Come on," Lydia motioned. "Let's go."

As the morning turned into the afternoon, the visiting room again filled to capacity. Annette joined some other small children in the play area, and Lydia introduced Kenny to some of the other kids who were visiting family members. "That's Oscar," she pointed at a boy about their age. "He hardly ever comes because he lives way down around Miami. He should be in fifth grade, but he flunked the third grade because of his FCAT scores." She rolled her eyes at Kenny when she said, "FCAT," the dreaded exams most Florida students were subjected to each year. Lydia seemed to know everyone's story, although she didn't spend a lot of time with anyone in particular. She paused for quick conversations as everyone caught up with each other. It was obvious that no one kept in touch outside of the prison visits, other than the brief emails he and Lydia had exchanged.

The kids in the visiting room reminded Kenny of when Gram took GiGi, her fat little dog with its cute-ugly face, to the fenced-in dog area at her condo. All of the dogs were quick to check each other out, but then they hurried on to something else of interest. So it was here. Greetings, brief interactions, and moving on.

"Hey, congratulations on the whole D.A.R.E. thing," Lydia said. "I almost forgot to ask you about that. What did you write about?" Kenny described his essay hoping he could explain it clearly.

"It sounds really good," Lydia said. "Email it to me so I can read it?" It was more of a request than a command.

"Sure. I'll email it tomorrow."

"Thanks! You're lucky you have writing talent. I can tell good stories, but I just can't write them down. I have no idea why that is. I just hate to sit and write. I'd rather talk." Lydia grinned at Kenny. "Yeah," she went on "sometimes I'm a real motor-mouth!"

Kenny laughed. Lydia was talkative, there was no doubt about that.

"Well, next time you get a writing assignment, you'll just have to tell the story out loud, but record it when you tell it. That way, you can play the tape back and copy it down. That's what Mrs. Juarez used to do with the students who didn't like to write, and now they're a lot better than they used to be." Kenny remembered Danny Fitzgerald coming in second in the essay contest. He was one of the students Mrs. Juarez had taught that strategy. It seemed to have worked.

"I'll try it sometime," Lydia said. "What I'd rather do instead of writing stories is to make movies. I almost went to a movie-making camp one summer, but it cost too much." Kenny looked up. He might be going to a writer's camp this summer. Should he tell Lydia, or would it sound like bragging?

"Yeah, that would be fun. One of my favorite books is *Making My Escape*, and it's all about this boy, Danny Finn, who is making a sci-fi movie with his friends. Well, that and the fact that his dad is a real jerk. So, the evil sci-fi character is really the dad. You'd like it. Especially the movie-making parts."

"It sounds good," Lydia said with interest. "Who wrote it?"

"David Finkle."

"Cool. Well, I'll have to see if it's in our media center. My mom's not too big on buying books when I can get them free at school."

"Yeah, I know. Mrs. Juarez has it in our classroom library. Let me know if you can't find it, and I'll ask if I can borrow hers. There's a lot of technical stuff about movie-making that you would probably like – storyboards? – and I know you'll like the plot and characters, too."

Kenny looked across the room. He saw Annette making her way towards Mom and Dad, probably wanting something else from the vending machines.

"Any news on your dad's and Hector's case?" Lydia asked bluntly. She was very comfortable with topics Kenny was just beginning to get used to. He took a deep breath and thought about it.

"Well," he confided, "my mom and Leticia are trying to find some help on a web site that helps inmates with legal things. My mom hasn't actually come out and told me the details, but I overheard her on the phone with my dad, and I also heard her talking to Leticia, so I know a little bit." Kenny glanced over at his parents who were deep in conversation. *They're probably talking about the same thing*, he thought.

"Apparently there is a lawyer who understands what happened, and, I'm not a hundred percent sure, but he might be able to get my dad and Hector a retrial, and they could get out of prison. But it's not a hundred percent, and no one has really told me anything." Kenny finished breathlessly, his words strung together almost as hurriedly as Gram's.

"Wow! That's great news!" Lydia's eyes widened. Then her face changed. "Listen, Kenny, don't take this wrong, okay? But I've been coming here for years, and I've heard so many stories about guys who are going to get out and stuff, but..." she hesitated, "you know, it doesn't seem to happen. Uh, much." She looked closely at Kenny hoping she hadn't offended him. He looked resigned.

"I know," he shook his head, "and I think that's why my mom isn't telling me anything, so I don't get my hopes up."

Lydia was relieved and launched into a self-rebuttal, "Yeah, but don't ever give up hope, 'cause it *does* happen! How about all that DNA evidence and stuff? You know? Guys are found innocent all the time with DNA testing."

"I know," he agreed, "I saw it on TV, and I saw it in the newspaper one day at school, but that's for murder cases." Kenny thought that Lydia flinched just a little. *Oh no*, he thought, *what if her dad is in for murder?* He still didn't know her dad's crime. It might have been his imagination, though, because she forged right ahead.

"Well, I know DNA won't help your dad, but you know, maybe the new trial or something will show how it wasn't even his car. You know – some new evidence or something." She spoke with conviction, and like someone who knew what it was like to wish and hope for such a turn of events.

"Yeah... well, I hope so. We'll see." Now Kenny sounded skeptical, like a grown-up promising a little kid she could take a trip on the space shuttle.

"Oh!" he exclaimed suddenly, turning towards Lydia. "I can't believe I forgot to tell you this! I heard my mom and Leticia talking. Guess who got arrested?"

"Len Herd?" Lydia couldn't imagine anyone else.

"Yep! He was stalking one of his ex-wives or something. Up in North Carolina, I think. Maybe now he'll finally go to prison where he belongs!" Kenny was jubilant. So was Lydia.

"Ha! Good! What a *creep*! Let's hope his lawyer doesn't get him off!" Lydia was in complete sympathy with Kenny when it came to Len Herd.

"Oh, and that's the other thing. There is a rumor that his attorney won't represent him. Conflict of interest or something. Or maybe because it happened in a different state. I don't know any of the details. Mom doesn't tell me. I'm not even sure she really knows everything herself."

"Wow! It sounds kind of promising, though, doesn't it?" Lydia and Kenny gloated over the news. Their camaraderie was even stronger when they were on this particular topic.

Annette wandered over. She was growing bored and restless, Kenny could tell. He looked up at the clock. No wonder! Visitation would soon be over. Where had the day gone?

"Kenny, do you have four quarters?" Annette had learned how to make a dollar with change.

"What do you want that costs a dollar?" Lydia asked.

"I don't know, but I'll look for something."

Kenny and Lydia laughed. Annette just wanted to spend a dollar.

"There won't be much left now," Kenny reminded her. "Let's go see."

The three of them walked to the vending machines, which were just about cleaned out. It reminded Kenny that the visit would soon be ending. He had spent a lot of the morning with his dad, telling him details about school that took too long for a phone conversation. Kenny understood that his parents needed time to talk alone, so he was grateful for Lydia's company. He imagined the same was true in her case, and he looked over at her parents. They seemed to be enjoying a relaxed conversation. He wondered again why Lydia's dad was in prison.

"I want that one," Annette pointed, breaking into Kenny's thoughts.

"Okay," Kenny replied, "which buttons will you have to press?"

Annette was ready. "B-6!"

"Sounds like a bingo game," Lydia joked.

Kenny put the quarters in the slot, Annette pressed the buttons, and down came her treat – a squashed cupcake-looking thing that didn't look very appetizing, which is probably why it was still here at the end of the day. Annette picked it up and examined it. She seemed to be making a judgment call.

"Put it back," she requested, handing the cupcakes to Kenny.

"No can do, amigo," Kenny told her. "This isn't Wal-Mart."

Annette reluctantly took the cupcakes and headed for the play area. Kenny imagined she was suddenly about to become generous. He and Lydia watched as Annette bent over another little girl who was helping her baby brother with something. Annette was clearly trying to pawn off the cupcakes.

"Ha! Ha!" Kenny and Lydia both laughed. "Maybe this time there really is something wrong with the food!" The two sat down again.

"So, we're almost out of here," Lydia said, looking at the clock. "What are you doing this week in school?" Here was Kenny's opportunity to tell Lydia his big news. She would know he wasn't trying to brag.

"Let's see, you know about the D.A.R.E. contest already." Lydia nodded. "Well, Mrs. Juarez talked to me on Friday about another opportunity. For writing. There's this summer program for kids at Stetson University – it's where she went to college to become a teacher. The program is called HATS – High Achieving Talented Students. H-A-T-S?" Lydia nodded again as she removed her headband and smoothed her hair before sliding it back on. "Mrs. Juarez said they have a lot of different courses, including creative writing. And this year there is a special program they're holding in Hannibal, Missouri. That's where Mark Twain grew up, so the idea is to go and stay in Hannibal for one week and see all the places that inspired Mark Twain, like the Mississippi River and the cave. You know, from *Tom Sawyer*?"

"Whoa, that is so cool! Are you going?"

"That's the part I don't know yet. It's for kids in fifth through eighth grade, so I'm eligible, but you have to send a sample of your best writing and see if you get accepted."

"Aw, you'll be accepted! How much does it cost?"

"Nothing. If they like my writing and I get accepted, it doesn't cost me anything. And I'll get to stay there for a whole week learning how to be a better writer, plus getting to see all the Mark Twain stuff. There's a girl in my class, Rachel Mason, who is crazy about Mark Twain. I don't know if Mrs. Juarez is encouraging her to go or not, but Rachel's a good writer, too."

"Can anyone send in a writing sample, or is it just for kids at your school?"

"It's for anyone in the right age group. And only twelve kids will get to go." As Kenny said this he suddenly realized that the odds were against him getting accepted. But he was going to try.

"When will you know?" Lydia pressed.

"I guess in plenty of time before summer. I have to ask Mrs. Juarez. I just found out about it two days ago. She seems to think I have a good chance." Kenny laughed. "Hey, maybe she can put in a good word for me since she graduated from Stetson, right?"

"Anything's possible. I think you're going to get it. I can feel it in my bones."

Kenny laughed. Lydia sounded like Gram now. He was glad he had told her. And he knew that if he did get to go to Hannibal, Missouri for a week to see where Mark Twain grew up, Lydia would be glad for him. He imagined himself sending her a postcard. Kenny would send his dad one, too. Then again, he hoped his dad would be set free by summer.
The signal came suddenly from the guard's desk. "The-following-visits-have-fifteen-minutes-remaining: Evans-O'Reilly-McAllister-Novak-Kirby-Coulter. Fifteen-minutes."

Kenny stood up to go sit with his dad and mom for a few minutes before the long drive home. Lydia's dad would be called in the next batch of inmates. He knew the routine now after just one visit. The two friends looked at each other for a moment.

"Email me!" Lydia said as she began to walk away. "Hey!" She stopped and turned around to face Kenny. "Are you coming up next Sunday?" Kenny looked over his shoulder at his parents who were saying their goodbyes to each other. He looked back at his new friend and smiled.

"Yep," Kenny assured her, "See you next Sunday." Then he saluted and turned away.

The end

Predict the Future

Kenny's story ends on a hopeful note, but what happens next? Does his dad get out of prison? Is Ron Evans found innocent? What about Len Herd? And what about Kenny? Will he get to go to the young authors program in Hannibal? And let's not leave out Lydia! Maybe she and Kenny will find themselves sharing further adventures. You are invited to predict their futures by visiting http://rachelmason.com where you can read what others have written about Kenny and his classmates.

Help and hope

Log on to http://rachelmason.com for useful information and the most current list of organizations that might be able to help kids like Kenny.

The Center for Children of Incarcerated Parents
http://www.e-ccip.org/index.html

Big Brothers, Big Sisters Organization
http://www.bbbs.org

About the Author

Cindy Lovell, author of *Rachel Mason Hears the Sound*, is an Associate Professor of Education at Quincy University in Quincy, Illinois. Her areas of expertise include gifted education, teaching English as a second language, and Mark Twain. Cindy has two grown children, Angela and Adam. She lives in Hannibal, Missouri where she directs the Mark Twain Young Authors Workshop.

Cindy can be reached through N.L. Associates for speaking engagements and workshop presentations.

N.L. Associates Inc.
PO Box 1199
Hightstown, NJ 08520-0399
732-605-1643
www.storieswithholes.com